White
Christmas
BRIDES

White Christmas BRIDES

Four Delightful
Historical Romances
to Warm the Heart

Diana Lesire Brandmeyer, Pam Hillman,
Susan Page Davis, Michelle Ule

BARBOUR BOOKS
An Imprint of Barbour Publishing, Inc.

The Festive Bride © 2014 by Diana Lesire Brandmeyer
The Christmas Tree Bride © 2014 by Susan Page Davis
The Evergreen Bride © 2014 by Pam Hillman
The Yuletide Bride © 2014 by Michelle Ule

ISBN 978-1-63058-935-6

Published by Barbour Books, an imprint of Barbour Publishing, Inc., P.O. Box 719, Uhrichsville, Ohio 44683, www.barbourbooks.com

Our mission is to publish and distribute inspirational products offering exceptional value and biblical encouragement to the masses.

ecpa Member of the
Evangelical Christian
Publishers Association

Printed in the United States of America.

The Festive Bride

By Diana Lesire Brandmeyer

Chapter 1

Southern Illinois 1886

Roy Gibbons stirred the pot of oatmeal while doing his best to ignore the state of his kitchen.

"Papa, it shouldn't look like that." Eight-year-old Elisbet glared at him. "I can't wait until our Christmas mama gets here."

If Janie were here, everything would be in the cupboards where they belonged, not shoved into nooks and crannies. He never thought he'd be making breakfast for his daughters, much less trying to keep their frocks clean and pressed. He missed his wife more and more every day. Roy didn't know how she'd made his home run so smoothly. Not once had he needed to worry about how to get tomato stains off his shirt or when to cut his hair. She'd say in her musical voice, "It's time, sit down and let me trim that head, Roy."

When Elisbet asked him for a mother for Christmas, he'd said yes, thinking it couldn't be that hard to find one.

"Papa, do you think Becky will have sugar cookies at her party?" Frances, his youngest and his shadow, tugged his pant leg.

"Franny, she's going to have cake. That's what you have at a birthday party, right, Papa?" Elisbet never had trouble correcting her younger sister.

"But I like sugar cookies." Frances tugged again. "Can we make cookies when we come home? Mama makes the best kind."

"Mama *made* not makes. She's in heaven. Remember?" Elisbet patted her sister's shoulder. "When our Christmas mama comes, she'll make cookies with us."

"Stop telling her that, Elisbet. It's not that easy to get a mother. I can't order one from the catalog." He slid the pot from the burner, his little shadow still clinging to his leg as he moved. "Sit down girls, and I'll fill your bowls." Roy was still stinging from Widow Percy's rejection. She'd have been a perfect fill-in for his deceased wife. Seemed logical—she didn't have a father for her boys, and his girls didn't have a mother. When he suggested they marry for the common good of their families, she'd done all but slapped his face.

Trouble was, he hadn't lived here long enough to know people. Maybe he'd made a mistake moving here after Janie died. If he'd had stayed in Collinsville, he'd have a mother for the girls by now. The whole reason he'd left was because too many young hopefuls were knocking on the door with some treat and mooning over him and the girls. At the time he didn't want another wife. No one could fill Janie's shoes, and these women would be expecting to have children of their own. He couldn't face that, not after losing Janie and the baby. No, he didn't need a companion. Just someone to take care of his house and his family.

He scooped up the oatmeal and plopped a lump in each girl's bowl.

He sat at the head of the table, a daughter on either side of him, and pushed back the hurt that came from seeing Janie's chair at the other end. The house was different, but the spot across the table was as empty as if he hadn't left Collinsville. "Grace, then food." He watched until little hands were folded and heads bowed, then said the prayer followed by an "Amen."

Frances stuck her fingers on the inside of her bowl to pull it closer. "Hot!" The bowl went spinning from the table to her lap and then crashed to the floor. She wailed.

"Are you all right? Are your fingers burned?" Roy sprung from his chair and pulled his daughter from hers. He grabbed her hands and flipped them palm up.

They weren't red. Relieved to avoid a crisis, he planted a kiss on her fingertips the way he'd seen Janie do so many times.

"My dress," Frances whimpered. "It's dirty. I don't have another one for the party."

"Shh, Frances, stop crying. Your fingers look fine, and no one will notice your dress." Kneeling, he reached under the table for the offending bowl and spoon that had spoiled Frances's morning.

"If we had a mama, this wouldn't have happened, Papa." Elisbet already held a wet rag in her hand. She dabbed at her sister's dress. "It's only a little bit of oatmeal. Look, Franny. See? I got it off."

It bothered him that Elisbet tried to be like Janie, and he had no idea how to prevent it.

"But it's my favorite and it's. . ." Frances hiccupped. "Wet!"

Roy wondered how he would ever raise these girls without help.

∞

Alma Pickens tugged her cape closer to guard against the sharp fangs of the November wind and leaned across the buggy seat. Her father had returned to the very subject she'd asked him not to speak about at breakfast. "Papa, you're a dreamer. Maybe I'm not the only one God will send a spouse for. I do believe I'll pray as hard as you do for me, that you'll marry again. A doctor should have a wife."

And she would take it to God in her prayers. She'd grown weary of her father's constant efforts to see her married. It wasn't that she was against the idea, but she'd made a promise to her mother to take care of him. And it would be a rare man who would marry her and take in her father as well.

Besides, she had her painting and taking care of her father's home. That gave her plenty to do. Why, just this morning she'd risen earlier than normal and put in a full day's work so she could come to town with him despite the cold to make a deposit at the bank and to visit her friend Jewel.

"Little Bit, it's not right for you to devote your life to me."

"Papa, I told you not to worry about me. I have you, and I don't need anyone else. Besides, there isn't anyone left in Trenton that I'd care to marry."

"Alma my girl, you'll make a good wife and mother. I can't sit back and watch you miss out. God will bring someone." He stopped the horse in front of Bossman's Bank and stepped out of the wagon. He tied the horse to the hitching post and helped Alma dismount. "I'm too old to get married again. It's you I worry about. I'll pick you up at Jewel's when I'm through at the Detterman's. And don't start making lists of promising wives for me. Go on, get in the bank and put your pennies away."

"I'm going." Who would be a good match for him? And who could she find that wouldn't mind her presence in the house as well?

Maybe she should hold off ordering from the Montgomery Ward catalog. She had her heart set on the Oil Painting Outfit Complete. It was outrageously expensive, but it came with twenty-five colors of paint. If she weren't able to sell her paintings right away, and her father married a woman who valued their privacy, she would need that money to rent a room somewhere. And without the paints and lessons that came with the painting outfit, how would she have anything to sell? Well, she wouldn't worry about that today, seeing as how there weren't any women who interested Papa. The irony that this town held no one for either of them struck her. Maybe Papa would consider moving to St. Louis, where her paintings would be discovered, and she'd be famous and wealthy. He could be a doctor there, and the number of people in that city would increase his chance of finding another wife.

She needed to talk this new idea of St. Louis over with Jewel. Together they'd find a solution.

∞

Inside the bank, Alma waited her turn. Two little blond girls in front of her clung to their father. She knew who they were—the Gibbons family minus the mother who had died last spring giving birth. Mrs. Remik at the store said everyone was speculating on when Mr. Gibbons would take another wife to help with Elisbet and Frances.

The oldest, Elisbet, played peekaboo with her sister. Their giggles captured one hiding in Alma. She clenched her lips to contain it, but it escaped.

Mr. Gibbons turned and smiled. Alma had an unusual urge to slide her finger into the indentation on his cheek. Dimples. Then she noticed what looked like oatmeal in his hair. She shuddered. The man needed help.

"I apologize if my girls disturbed you, miss."

"They didn't. Their giggles captivated me along with those dark blue eyes." If she were painting them, she'd use cobalt blue to capture their intensity.

"We're going to a birthday party," Elisbet said.

Alma leaned down. "I love birthday parties, lots of games and cake to eat."

"I have oatmeal on my dress." Frances looked so sorrowful that Alma wanted to take her down to the store and buy her a new frock.

"Franny, it's okay. Remember I got it off and your dress dried on the way here. Papa, we have to get Becky a gift, don't forget. I want to get her red hair ribbons."

Had that man brought his daughter out in this cold weather with a wet dress? Was he touched in the head? No doubt her own father would end up at their place tending to the little girl for pneumonia.

"I don't. I think we should get her a knife." Frances held up her hands and pretended to open one. "It would be grand to have one. Papa, can I have one for my birthday?"

"We'll see. We best get moving if there's shopping and lunch to do yet." He turned to Alma. "Nice to meet you."

"Papa, can she be the mama you're getting us for Christmas? She doesn't have a wedding ring. I looked like you showed me." Elisbet smiled a got-you-now smile at her father.

Mr. Gibbons's green eyes flashed to Alma's, and his face flushed. "Let's go, girls." He ushered them out without another word to Alma.

Alma watched them leave, noticing the hem on

Elisbet's coat was torn. She understood the child's desire for a mother but sincerely hoped her father didn't run into Mr. Gibbons before Christmas.

Chapter 2

Roy covered Frances's shivering body with the blanket from his bedroom and tucked it around her. Her teeth chattered and he brushed his hand against her forehead. Hot. Nothing good ever came from fevers. He couldn't let his daughters see his worry, especially Elisbet. "You'll be right as rain soon. I sent Pete to fetch the doctor. He'll be here before long."

"Not the doctor!" Frances sobbed. "I want Mama."

Her words cut him, opening a scar he'd thought healed. "We all do. The doctor will help you feel better, sweetheart." He'd taken to calling his daughters by the terms of endearment he'd heard Janie use. It seemed to settle them down when they were in a state he didn't understand. He should never have left Collinsville. Right now his mother could be helping him with this sick child.

Frances coughed again and again. Her body shook, and her chest had a rattle Roy didn't like. "Elisbet, sit and read to your sister until the doctor and Pete get here or I get done milking the cows."

Elisbet, eyes wide and face pale, didn't object, but grabbed the picture book Frances loved. "Can I get under the covers with Franny?"

"I want Elisbet!" Frances threw off the covers.

Frances didn't know what she wanted, but he would give her what he could. "Didn't I just tuck you in, little girl?"

"Please, Papa?" Frances coughed again.

Roy slid back the covers. "Climb in." He waited for Elisbet to snuggle in next to her sister. *Please God, don't let her get sick, too.* "I'll be back as soon as I can."

Roy knew Elisbet was terrified. He wished he didn't understand her fear, but he did—all too well. The last time they'd seen a doctor, Janie died. He left his heart with his daughters as he headed outside. You couldn't let a cow go unmilked, even if you had somewhere better to be.

He shivered. He should have grabbed his coat. No matter, the barn would hold back the chill. He'd have to keep Elisbet home from school tomorrow to help him with Frances. He couldn't take care of a sick child, do barn chores, and work at the mill. This illness pushed him to fulfill his daughters' Christmas wish. He'd write to his mother, asking her who back home was still looking to get married. He wanted a widow, someone who'd already known love and didn't expect it to happen again. Someone who'd understand she couldn't replace his wife any more than he could replace her husband.

∽∞∾

Alma convinced her father to take her for an afternoon drive before the winter snows came and forced them to stay close to town. Outside of town, the roads suffered from last week's gully washer, making the smooth rides of summer a memory to be cherished. The buggy springs bounced, squeaking as the wheels dipped in and out of holes in the dirt road. Alma held on to the edge of her seat. "Thanksgiving makes me sad. It makes me think of Mama."

"I think about her every day. Holidays are the hardest for me. But you've your mother's happy attitude about life, and that helps me." Her father winked at her. "Yes, you do many things that remind me of her."

"Tell me how, Papa." Alma drew the buggy blanket up higher on her lap. The warmth of fall had been shoved aside as winter gained a foothold. The trees held tight to a few weather-beaten leaves. Another strong wind and they'd be bare.

"The way you want to make small things into a celebration. Like Thursday, you invited friends to eat with us, but it wasn't enough to have all those platters of food. You decorated the table with red and gold leaves. That's not something I would do."

"Too many germs, Dr. Pickens? Those tiny little things no one can see?" Alma tried to raise an eyebrow the way her father did when making a point. It wouldn't go.

Dr. Pickens raised his brow. "Still can't do it? Neither could your mother. And yes, there is a new study out about germs being in unexpected places. It's possible leaves would carry bacteria spores, but your happiness matters more to me, so I kept quiet."

"Thank you. The decorations made the entire dinner party more festive. If the leaves make people sick, wouldn't everyone be ill when they fall from the trees?"

"It does seem I have more patients in the winter, doesn't it?"

"That's because it's cold, and we don't get enough fresh air. You taught me that. So I'm like you, too, Papa."

"I'd like you to be more like your mother and me—married."

This conversation was going down a corduroy road she didn't wish to travel. Distraction always worked with her father. "Who was the letter from that you were reading last night?"

"Someone you don't know. How about Mr. Bruin? He'd make a good husband."

"I can't marry him. I won't. I know you're concerned for me, but I'd never be happy married to a miner. I'm surprised you would even consider him. He must bring home lots of germs every night. Why, I could catch something and die before spring if I were to marry him." She tried one more time to arch her eyebrow. It wouldn't go, so she pushed it up with her finger.

In the distance, Alma saw a horse and a rider coming up on them fast. "Look, someone else is out for a ride today."

"Doesn't appear he's riding for fun. Must be an emergency. He's got that horse running at a gallop." Dr. Pickens pulled back on the reins. "Wise to slow down and let him pass. No need to give our boy Charlie here a reason to bolt."

The horseback rider whipped off his hat and waved. "Dr. Pickens! We need you at the Gibbons'." He stopped his horse next to the buggy.

"Pete, you came up so fast I didn't recognize you. What's the problem?"

"Roy Gibbons's little one is sick. She can't stop coughing, and he said she's burning hot as a barn afire. He sent me to get you. Can you come straight away?"

Her father wore his serious face; she knew he wouldn't hesitate.

"We'll follow you." Doctor Pickens urged Charlie into a trot.

"What does Mr. Gibbons do for a living, Papa?"

"I heard he bought Becker's farm." His forehead furrowed like a freshly plowed field.

"He's not married. Jewel says he never comes to town without the girls. Why do you suppose that is?"

"I take you places."

"Yes, but not all the time. Do you think he's taking care of the girls by himself? That would explain the oatmeal in his daughter's hair and the torn hem."

"Oatmeal? What are you talking about?"

"I saw them at the bank. The girls were going to a birthday party and were excited, but they weren't dressed for a party. I wanted to take them home, curl their hair, and buy them pretty dresses. I hope the other children weren't mean to them."

"Were they mean to you?" Her father's mouth turned down.

She hadn't meant to hurt him. "No. Well, sometimes. It didn't happen after you asked for help from Mrs. Wilson."

"She was a saint to step in. I'm not sure you would

have learned how to be a lady if not for her."

"You tried, Papa." Alma pushed back memories of the times she missed her mother. She'd kept many of them from her father.

The two-story farmhouse appeared when they came around the bend in the road. A house built for a large family, not a father and two little girls. "Will you let me help?"

"Don't believe you've become a doctor since lunch, have you?"

"No."

"You can carry my bag."

"I'm no longer a child."

"Believe me, I'm aware."

The door opened, and Mr. Gibbons stepped onto the porch. "In here, Doctor. Franny is sick. I don't know what to do."

Alma followed her father into the house. She'd learned early to step back when her father was needed. Too many times she'd landed on the floor as he rushed by her.

Mr. Gibbons hadn't waited for either of them, but it wasn't difficult to locate him or the patient. The coughing led them to the sick child.

Dr. Pickens felt Frances's forehead. "Definitely a

fever. You need to take those blankets off of her right now. You're making the fever climb higher. I need a basin of cold water and a cloth, please."

When Mr. Gibbons removed the covers, Frances cried out. "I'm cold!"

Alma rushed to the child's side and stroked her arm. "Do you like to build snowmen? I bet you're as cold as one, aren't you?"

Frances quieted. "Yes."

"Mr. Gibbons, the water please?" Papa dug in his black bag. It was a good thing he'd acquired the habit of tossing it into the buggy whenever he left home.

Alma spoke to Mr. Gibbons. "I'll watch over her while you're gone. It won't take but a minute to get what Papa needs."

He nodded and hastened from the room. Alma felt compassion for the man. Not having a wife to help him through this trying time had to be difficult.

"I'm cold."

"Keeping the covers on will make you sicker longer. Then you'll be sad if it snows and you can't go outside to build a snowman." Alma sat on the bed next to Frances and picked up a book. "Were you reading this?"

"Sissy read it to me."

"Where is Sissy?"

Frances pointed to the corner where Elisbet stood, her eyes focused on Alma's father. She seemed frozen in fear.

Alma smoothed Frances's hair. "My papa will take good care of you. Right now, I'm going to talk to Sissy." She went to Elisbet and knelt in front of her.

She grasped the child's hand. "You don't need to be afraid. My papa is a good doctor. He can make your sister well. Do you want to watch?"

Elisbet yanked her hand away, eyes wide. "No! She's going to die like Mama."

❦

"No, she's not going to die." Roy strode into the room in time to hear Elisbet. "Right, Doc? Tell them everything is going to be fine." *Tell me, too.* He couldn't bear losing Frances. *God, please don't take her, too.* He'd been praying for her to get better. But then, he'd prayed for Janie, and it didn't make a difference.

Dr. Pickens removed the stethoscope from around his neck and returned it to his bag. "She'll be fine. She's got the croup. Feed her soup and give her tea with honey to soothe her throat and cough. I have a tincture you'll need to give her three times a day."

"Will Elisbet catch this, too?" If both girls were sick, he wouldn't be able to work at the mill. As it was, the idea of leaving Elisbet alone with Franny caused him some concern.

"She might. If she does, follow the same procedure. Keep a cool cloth on Frances's forehead for the night. Dip it in cold water when it warms. That will help bring down her fever. Keep her in bed for a few days."

"I don't have to go to school?" Frances propped herself up on her elbows.

"Then I'm not going either." Elisbet strutted from the corner. "I'll take care of Franny."

"We'll discuss it when the doctor has gone."

"Mr. Gibbons, do you have someone to watch the girls?" Dr. Pickens asked. "They are too small to stay home alone."

"I don't have a choice. You don't understand. It's the three of us that looks out after each other."

"I'll watch them."

He turned and noticed the doctor's daughter was the woman from the bank. She held Elisbet's small hand in hers. It took him back in time. Janie with her daughters. Would it hurt them to have another woman look after them? Would they become attached, or worse, badger her about marrying him?

"Please, Papa?"

"Pretty please, Papa?"

Roy rubbed his forehead. He needed help. He'd deal with the consequences later.

Chapter 3

Alma's father waited in the buggy at the Gibbons farm. The sun cracked open the morning sky. Alma had brought fresh eggs, since she wasn't sure what their pantry held.

Mr. Gibbons met her with a finger over his lips. "They're still sleeping." He yawned. "Sorry, I was up most of the night."

"Is Frances better? Papa wants to know before he drives back to town."

"I think so. She doesn't feel as hot this morning, and she's not restless."

She turned and waved to her father. He tipped his hat in her direction and jiggled the reins. Charlie shook his head, pawed the ground, and the buggy wheels turned.

She didn't smell coffee brewing. "You haven't eaten?"

"No, you woke me up. It's a good thing, too. I need to do the barn chores first. I would have been late to work if you hadn't come when you did."

Alma held out the basket she'd brought along. "I brought eggs. If you don't mind, I can make breakfast." She didn't think twice about offering, but the grin on Mr. Gibbons's face said she'd given him a large gift.

"You wouldn't mind?" He was already sticking his arms into his coat sleeves.

"Not at all." Especially if he kept flashing those dimples at her.

"None of us are too picky about food. If you can make the oatmeal, I'd appreciate it." He took off out the door.

The minute she walked into the kitchen, Alma knew Mr. Gibbons didn't have a woman helping him. The stove was filthy, and there were dishes caked with dried oatmeal stacked on the table. She shrugged off her cloak and searched for an apron. Mr. Gibbons had left a shirt draped over a chair. With a sigh, she tied the sleeves around her waist. Not the best use of a shirt, but maybe it would save her favorite day dress.

She stoked the stove and put on the coffee. Next, she gathered the dirty dishes and put them in the sink to soak. She hadn't had breakfast either, and she hated oatmeal. There had to be something else for her to make that would be easy for Frances to eat. A quick search of the food supply, and she had the makings for griddle cakes. The syrup would go down Frances's throat easier than lumpy oatmeal.

She found a clean bowl and mixed the ingredients.

"What are you doing?" Elisbet, hair tousled and in her nightclothes, peeked around the corner.

"Griddle cakes. Do you and your sister like them?"

"Better than oatmeal." Elisbet skipped across the floor. "Can I help?"

"Can you get out the griddle for me?"

Elisbet disappeared into the pantry and brought out the heavy cast-iron piece. "I can grease it. Mama showed me how."

"That would be helpful, thank you. Before you do that, could you get dressed and check to see if your sister is awake?"

"She's sleeping, but I bet she wakes up when she smells these cooking. Don't grease it, promise?"

"I promise. Off you go, and put on some warm clothes. It's cold today."

While the batter was resting, Alma started cleaning. She was wiping down the table when Mr. Gibbons came in the back door.

"Thanks for starting breakfast. I can finish up."

"I'm making griddle cakes, not oatmeal."

His dimples came out to torment her again. She

needed a diversion. "Why don't you check on Frances? See if you can get her to come to breakfast?"

"You have flour on your face." Mr. Gibbons reached over and brushed her cheek then withdrew his fingers fast, as if he'd been burnt. He whirled around and headed for the bedroom, muttering something about checking on Frances.

Alma touched her cheek where his fingers had been. If she were made of butter, she'd be a puddle on the floor.

❧

Next to the window in her bedroom sat Alma's art studio. She'd tried to capture the playfulness of the barn kittens from last spring. The laundry basket looked right, but the kittens in it were giving her a great amount of difficulty. Jewel had been instrumental in helping her find an outlet for her creativity after her attempt at weaving palm leaves together to make hats failed.

Would it be easier painting children? Frances and Elisbet would make good subjects, with their big blue eyes and blond curls. Curls that were a mess. After she'd cleaned the kitchen to a tolerable standard, she'd spent the rest of the day with the girls. She'd combed and braided their hair, even found ribbons to tie at the ends.

Their imaginations sparked hers, and they made up

stories of castles and trolls. She could feel how they wanted her attention, and she was happy to give it. She prayed Elisbet's Christmas wish would come true, and they would get a mother.

Splat. Black paint hit the canvas in the wrong spot and tailed like a tear. She ought not be thinking of those little ones. God would see to them. After all, He'd helped her father take care of her.

As the sun set, the light faded from golden to silver, making it difficult to see. Alma set her paintbrush and palette on the table next to her easel. Time to stop for today, which, by the look of the work she had accomplished this afternoon, was a good thing. Kittens shouldn't have cone-shaped heads, but she couldn't quite get them more rounded. Frustrated, she removed her painting apron and draped it over the chair. She had to get that painting kit and discover how to do it correctly.

Heavyhearted, she headed to the kitchen. On Wednesdays she always made stew. Papa made calls that day and was often late to dinner, which gave her time to work on her art.

She couldn't let the problem of the kittens' misshapen heads alone. How did other painters get those round shapes? How did they paint children's heads?

Did they trace something until they learned to do it freehanded? Maybe she could use one of her mother's china cups. But would a real artist resort to something so amateur? She would ponder that. Maybe for this painting it would be okay. The next time she saw Jewel, she'd inquire about the rules. She was determined to be a real artist, not just occupy her time, even though that's what Papa said she was doing.

Her shoulders drooped. If this painting didn't sell, he would surely start talking about husbands again. He'd given her three choices and asked her to pick one. She shuddered. She'd known all of them since grade school and had never been fond of any of them.

She gave the stew a quick stir. The kitchen felt closed in and dark this evening. There were so many things she wanted to do in here. Despite being dirty, the Gibbons' kitchen was cheerful and full of light. Jewel had painted candlesticks with sunflowers in her kitchen and planned to paint her hutch with flowers. It was time to broach the topic with Papa again about brightening up this room. Could she convince him to let her paint the corner cabinet?

He hated change. If you asked her, he lived too much in the past. Mama wasn't going to come back to life and complain about the look of the kitchen. Not when she was living in heaven, where everyone knew Christ had built her a mansion. Mama must love it there, all those bright colors and the sparkles on the streets. It was a shame they couldn't experience a bit of that here at home.

"It's time for a change. I'll tell him right after supper. I live here, too, and since neither of us is getting married and I do the cooking, the kitchen is as good as mine." Her hand flew to her mouth. Had she said that out loud? It was a good thing Papa wasn't lurking around the corner. He'd think she was daft. No, best find a way to ease into this change. He was a stubborn man, set in his ways, and his rules applied in this house. Maybe she should go to St. Louis on her own and take painting classes. That's what Jewel suggested, but Alma couldn't leave. Not when she'd promised to watch over him. Which brought her back to her plan of finding Papa a wife.

❧

Alma stirred the stew again. Papa was late, and she didn't know if she should continue to keep the food warm. Sometimes when he stayed out this long, the family that needed him fed him.

The back door creaked open, and she spun around. The air rushed in, making the kerosene flames dance in their glass, casting graceful shadows across the room. "Papa, you're so late. What happened? Did you deliver a baby?"

"Not tonight. Is supper still warm?"

"Yes, but I do believe I'll warm it a bit more for you."

"Not too long, I'm hungry. Been looking forward to a hearty meal tonight." Papa took off his coat, slung it over his bent arm, and grabbed his hat. "I'll put these away later." He dropped them on a kitchen chair and sat at the table. "How was your afternoon?"

Papa asking about her day before eating sent a shiver up Alma's back. He was up to something. Food always came before conversation. She turned to face him. "You know that it's painting day. Are you getting too old to remember? It's a good thing you have me around to help you through your days."

He had the grace to flush and bend his head. Yes, there was something he was about to say, and Alma knew she wouldn't like it.

"Don't sass me, Alma. I was being polite."

"I'm sorry, Papa. I was teasing. Your last call must have been difficult. You haven't complained about my joshing with you in a long time. Did you lose a patient? Would you like me to make you some cocoa?"

"Forgive me for snapping at you. It's been a long day." He scrubbed his hands across his face. "There's something I need to tell you, and I know you won't like it, but what's done is done. We'll discuss it later, after I've eaten."

Alma slid a plate of stew across the table in front of her father and took a seat. "What do you mean, it's done? And what does it have to do with me?"

Chapter 4

What's done is done? Inside Alma, tension built like steam collecting in a covered pot of boiling water. If Papa didn't finish his stew soon, she was going to snatch it off the table. How dare he drop a loaded statement that begged for questions and then say he'd discuss it with her as soon as he'd finished his supper? For once she was glad she hadn't remembered to make the biscuits.

Chew and swallow, her father ate slower than a snake swallowing a mouse. "Papa, can't you tell me anything?"

Dr. Pickens held up a finger and shook his head no.

Alma jumped from her chair. "I don't understand why you would keep something from me. It must be unpleasant, or you would have told me straight away. This isn't like you." She tugged her ear.

"Don't pull on your ear."

Her hand dropped to her side. It had taken her years to break that tugging habit, and with one sentence Papa brought back her insecurities.

"You'll know soon enough. I want to eat and think about how I want to say what I have to say."

"Eat faster, please, because I'm imagining all kinds of things." Alma paced the kitchen, which gave her no satisfaction, since it only took four steps to cross the room. She slid back into her chair, propped her elbows on the table, and then rested her chin on her palms. Fine. She'd wait him out by staring at him.

He didn't look her in the eye or tell her to remove her elbows from the table. Alma refused to change her position. Even if it wasn't working, it made her feel like she was doing something.

When the last bit of stew disappeared, Alma grabbed the bowl. "Let me put this in the sink."

Her father squinted at her then frowned. "Why do you have feathers in your hair?"

"I was creating a new hair ornament."

"Did you glue them in?"

"No, I glued them to a leather strip, but the glue wasn't quite dry and some of the feathers stuck. I'll get them out. Like most of the things I attempt to create, this was a failure, but I'm not giving up my creative works. Are you ready to tell me what you mean by 'what's done is done'?"

Dr. Pickens wiped his chin with a napkin and scooted

his chair away from the table. "I've made a decision. I've signed up for a surgical course in St. Louis."

"St. Louis!" Alma clapped her hands. "That's wonderful! It will be a perfect place for us to live. Why, Jewel and I were discussing this on Saturday. When do we have to leave?"

"I'm leaving at the end of the year. You aren't."

"I don't understand."

"You can't go with me. I'm renting a room by the school."

"How long will you be gone? You don't need to worry. I can watch over the house."

"No, you can't. I've rented it out. I'll be gone a year, and you, my dear, will be getting married before I leave."

Anger chased fear down her back like a cat running over piano keys. "Married? Who to? Papa! This is so wrong. I don't want to get married, you know that."

"So you've said. It's my job as a father to make sure you are taken care of, and that's what I've done."

"Who did you pick? The man who works at Bassler Brewery and stumbles home at night? The coal miner who coughs so much he's probably going to die soon? Or the man who beats his dog?"

"Daughter, I listened to you."

His forehead wrinkled the way it did when he was

concerned for her. Could it be he would change his mind? Alma stacked reasons why she needed to go with him to St. Louis, ready to use them all. "Good, then let's put this leaving me behind business away. There will—"

"Stop. I'm not finished. Yes, your reasons were sound for not picking one of those men. I've found a better one. Roy Gibbons. He's a good family man and goes to church. With Pastor Elrich's help, I obtained his mother's address. She wrote back. He's a good man and moved here to remove himself from memories of his deceased wife. The two of you are well-suited. We've shaken hands. There will be a marriage."

◦◦◦

Roy had hoped the dishes he'd tossed in to soak after dinner would clean up quick. He was wrong. Dried food seemed to have planted roots in the stoneware. He noticed the kitchen had lost the appetizing appeal it had held after Alma had cleaned it.

He used a knife to scratch the surface of the plate. Marrying Alma would solve quite a few problems. She wasn't a widow, but she seemed to like Elisbet and Frances. They'd taken to her, too. He could keep his Christmas promise to them. That made him smile. He'd wanted to tell them tonight, but decided to wait until after Dr. Pickens talked to Alma.

As far as he was concerned, a quick trip to see the minister after work one day next week would work out well. They'd be married, and Alma could start helping out right away. He'd already been through the courting of a woman and a wedding. He paused his chipping at the dried food. It had been nice the first time, but now it would be a waste of time. He and Alma would get to know each other after they were married.

Unless she expected to be courted. Her father had avoided that question when Roy brought it up. He'd said, "Alma will be happy to get married. She knows the little ones need a mother's care as soon as possible."

Seems her mother had died when she was a youngun. He went back to prying off the dried eggs. Roy figured God had sent him to Trenton because He knew Alma was here. That had to be it. A woman as pretty as she should be married by now, with children of her own.

Why wasn't she? Was there something wrong with her? Maybe she was too picky in who she wanted to marry? Add that to her father being willing to let her get married without a courting period.

It had been his experience with Janie that women didn't always say what they wanted. Perhaps this Alma was different? She must be, or her father wouldn't be so confident in arranging this marriage without talking to her first.

༒

"All you have is the word of his mother? What mother would say anything bad about her son?" Alma sucked in her anger.

"You might have a point about that, but like I said, I've seen how he treats his daughters. I figure how he takes care of them is a good indication of what he'll be like as a husband."

"So I can go around with dried oatmeal in my hair and the hem of my dress torn and dragging in the streets?"

"Alma, calm down. You'll fix those things as their mother. What I see is the way he gets them candy at the store, the way the littlest one hangs onto his pants leg and he doesn't mind. The oldest holds his hand while they walk into church."

"So as long as I have candy, hang on his pants leg, and hold his hand, I'll be treated special as his wife?"

"Alma Gail Pickens. Enough. The matter is settled. He'll be over here tomorrow to discuss the details with you. I've given my word that you'll marry him, and there won't be a fuss about not having a season of courting."

"And I have no say in this? I'm to marry him without knowing him? Without being in love?"

"There isn't time for courting. I'm leaving the day after Christmas, and I want this settled before then." Dr. Pickens reached across the table for his daughter's hand. "I promise, you'll grow to love each other."

Tears stung her eyes. "But I promised Mama that I'd take care of you."

"I know, and you have done that longer than you should. Mr. Gibbons is a good man and needs help. You saw that, you even told me about the sad state of his home and how his daughters are taken with you."

"That doesn't mean he's the marrying kind!" She yanked her hand away from him and pushed back her chair. Married by Christmas might be what her father and Mr. Gibbons wanted, but not her.

"You know that's false, Alma. Think about what you're saying. He's been married before, and from what I can tell, still loves his wife. That means a lot to me. I'm glad. I feel good about handing you over to him."

"Glad? You're glad about giving me to a man who still loves another?"

"Yes, to me it means he's wanting to have the same kind of comfort and companionship he had before."

"Does that mean you didn't love Mama enough to

want to marry again?"

"No, it means I never found someone I could love as much. Roy Gibbons has."

"I don't believe that. I won't do it." She snatched up the stew pan and scraped the metal spoon against the sides, not caring how much noise it made. She pushed the scraps into the garbage pail. She wasn't saving any leftovers. As far as she was concerned, Papa could make his own dinner from now on. See how glad he'd be about that.

Chapter 5

Roy thought it best to meet with Miss Pickens without his daughters. He'd left them with Pete, his farmhand. To their delight, Pete promised to take them out to play with the barn cats. They were so excited they forgot to ask where he was going and why they couldn't come with him. Even Frances had let go of his leg and attached herself to Pete.

Doctor Pickens's two-story brick home was much nicer than his. Guess it made sense to be located close to town where most of the people lived, quicker to get to emergencies. He raised his hand to knock on the door and then lowered it. Maybe this wasn't a good idea. It seemed reasonably sound yesterday, but now that he'd slept on it, the idea of marrying so quick felt wrong. His shoulders tightened. He and Miss Pickens would benefit from this arrangement. But would she like living on a farm so far from town? In a house that seemed too small when Frances and Elisbet got to squealing and shrieking? He'd given the doc his word though, so he best follow through. He and Miss

Pickens wouldn't be the first couple necessity had brought to the altar.

He tapped on the door, deciding a polite knock would be best. He stepped back and waited.

Miss Pickens opened the door. "Mr. Gibbons."

"Miss Pickens, your father suggested we meet this evening."

"Yes, he did."

Wasn't she going to ask him inside? "May I come in?"

She swung the door wide. "Please do. Papa is in the kitchen."

He'd remembered her blond hair and that's about all. When she'd rescued him during Frances's illness, he hadn't noticed her dark blue eyes or how the top of her head didn't come up to his shoulder. "I came to see you, not him."

"Perhaps you did, but since the two of you have arranged my life for me, you might as well work out the details and fill me in later." She turned, back straight, and walked away from him like royalty. "Shut the door behind you."

So this wouldn't be as easy as the doc suggested. Miss Pickens would be a challenge. He closed the door, and for the first time in quite a while found himself excited about the prospect of winning a woman's attention.

❧

Alma, still spitting mad, led Mr. Gibbons into the kitchen where her father waited. "Mr. Gibbons is here. I think you two should chat and then let me know when I'm to leave the house."

"Alma, that's not how this is going to work. I know you're angry, but sit and get to know him before you stomp upstairs." Dr. Pickens pulled out a chair for her. "Evening, Roy."

"Doc." Roy stooped his shoulders to get though the doorway.

Alma hadn't noticed before how tall he stood or the width of his chest. The man and his dimples took her breath away. Maybe it wouldn't be so bad being married to him. At least she'd have something worth looking at every day. She found her way to the chair her father stood behind, and sat. "Thank you. How are the girls?"

Roy sat across the table from her. "They're fine. Pete's letting them play with the barn cats while I'm here."

"What do they think of you getting married?" She heard the terse tone in her voice and didn't like it. She'd been taught better than this. "Love your neighbor as yourself" came to mind.

Dr. Pickens slid a cup of coffee onto the table in front of Mr. Gibbons and gave Alma a look she knew too well as he handed her one. She had taken this as far as she could.

"I know they are anticipating a mother for Christmas, so I wondered about their excitement at the news." There, that was better.

"I haven't told them. Thought I ought to talk to the woman I was marrying first and make sure there would be a wedding." He gave her a slow grin then took a sip of his drink.

He'd considered her feelings? Her heart fluttered. She hadn't expected that. "I don't understand. I thought..."

"Well, I agreed to marry you, but not until after I decided you would be interested. I can't be bringing home just anyone to be a mother to my daughters. There's enough fairy tales out there to scare them without getting them their own wicked stepmother."

"But..."

"Sorry, Miss Pickens, I didn't mean to imply that you would be like that. I think it best for both parties to be agreeable to marriage." He set his cup down. "What about you?"

Alma's tongue-twisted words couldn't make it past her lips. He had to be the most beautiful man she'd ever been this close to. She wrenched herself out of an imaginary embrace and felt the loss. "I—I think...yes."

Mr. Gibbons slapped his hands together, making her jump. "Then we have a deal. You're right, Doc, she did say yes."

Alma gasped.

"I talked to the reverend, and we can get married Sunday, Miss Pickens."

"No!" Alma's stomach contents slid and jerked, bumping into her throat. "Not Sunday. I have a few things to say about this wedding, and the first thing is—it won't be this weekend."

ᏗᎾᏗ

Roy couldn't be more confused. The woman had said she'd marry him. Why would she want to delay? Her father had said courting her wasn't necessary.

"Mr. Gibbons, I will marry you on Christmas Eve."

"Why wait? Four weeks isn't going to change any-thing, and I need a wife now."

"I refuse to be a replacement for your wife. I know you still love her, and I think that's admirable."

He felt his head nodding and wondered where this would go.

"Here are my demands. If I'm to be thrown into a marriage by my father's wishes, you will have to court me until we get married. It's the only wedding I intend to have, and I'm not going to walk into this one on Sunday, get up on Monday and make your breakfast and clean your house without some kind of happy memory to cling to."

"Demands?" He shoved his chair away from the table. "I don't—"

"Alma, I told you to give it time, and you'll fall in love with each other."

"You told her that, Doc? How can you promise her that?"

"Papa, it may or may not happen, and that's the way life is. Mr. Gibbons needs a mother for his girls more than he needs a wife, so I'm willing to do that. Before that happens, though, I want to be treated special. Right now, I feel like Mr. Gibbons ordered me from a catalog. He knows nothing about me or I him. It's only fair that I get to know him before we get married. I'm not asking for a year, only four weeks."

Miss Pickens had a good point. Roy settled his back against the chair. "What do you have in mind?"

"I'll make a list and give it to you when you pick me up for our first outing. You can choose where to take me." She rose from her chair and nodded. "This time tomorrow would be fine, unless you care to provide dinner?"

Roy's lips moved, though his mind couldn't grasp what he was saying. "Dinner. Yes, we have to eat."

"Tomorrow, then. Let me walk you to the door. I know you're needed at home, and I must work on my list."

Before he knew what had happened, Roy found himself escorted out by the pretty and spirited woman and left standing on the porch. How had she done that? Small as she was, he'd been moved to the door and hadn't felt a thing.

Chapter 6

Alma checked the mirror again for stray hairs that may be out of place. She wouldn't admit it to anyone, but she was excited to be seeing Mr. Gibbons. Her cheeks couldn't hide that, flushed as they were against her pale skin.

Should she be waiting for him when he arrived or make him wait a little bit? She missed her mother. Her papa did his best, but when it came to being a female, he was lost.

Making him wait didn't feel comfortable. She should have asked Jewel what to do. She picked up the list, folded it, and stuck it in her dress pocket.

Her dress. Was it all right? She didn't put on her fanciest one, but picked the blue wool one. It kept her warm, and Papa said it made her eyes bright as a July sky.

In the parlor, she settled on a chair. Papa had started a fire. He'd come home early to see her off. Most likely to make sure she would go with Mr. Gibbons.

"You look nice, my dear." Papa walked across the room and stoked the fire. "Mr. Gibbons should be here soon."

"Are you sure about this marriage, Papa? It's not too late. We haven't told anyone."

"I am."

"I understand you don't want me to come with you to St. Louis and you rented out my home, but I could stay with Jewel and her husband. Or perhaps one of the widows from church? It's only for a year."

"No. I considered those things, but it's not fair to you. Suppose I find a wife in St. Louis? Then what will you do? You need your own home and family. A place where you can paint the furniture if you want to."

"I don't have to change things," Alma whispered.

"I want the best for you." He dabbed his eye and turned back to the fire.

Footsteps landed heavy on the wooden porch. There was a pause, then a knock. He was here. Why did her heart flip like a griddle cake? Goodness, she would need to get this emotion controlled before she faced him.

"That's your intended. I'll get the door, you wait here. A little bit of mystery is a good thing. Your mother told me that. Guess I should have mentioned a few of those bits of wisdom to you sooner."

"There's still time, Papa."

"I love you, Little Bit. Don't forget that ever." He gave her a quick hug and released her.

"I won't. You're making me cry. My face will be all red."

"You're beautiful, like your mother." He stepped out of the room.

Alma blinked and looked at the ceiling to keep the tears from falling. She turned to see Mr. Gibbons standing in front of her father. He smiled. She caught the schoolgirl sigh before it escaped.

⤬

Roy had cleaned the carriage the best he could in the cold weather. He didn't think Miss Pickens would notice, but she sure would if it were a mess. "I hope you don't mind. We'll be dining at my house tonight. The girls are excited that you'll be eating with us." More than that, they'd been collecting pinecones after school and arranging them multiple ways across the tabletop.

"We're eating at your house?" Alma pivoted to look at him.

"That's what I said. The girls helped me set the table, even made some decorations, though I told them it's not a holiday."

"Nothing wrong with expressing creativity. It will be fun to see what they've come up with. Did they collect things from inside or outside?"

"You'll have to wait and see. They like you—the girls."

"I like them, too." She rubbed her hands together.

"Are you cold? I have a blanket if you need it." He reached behind her, brought it over the carriage seat, and handed it to her.

Alma covered her lap and stuck her hands underneath. "Thank you. I should have brought my muff, but I didn't want to give into it being winter yet. I dread its full-blown arrival."

"There, I've learned something about you. Winter is not your favorite season."

"I didn't say that. I love snow and ice skating, but the season lasts too long."

"I can never decide. In the heat of summer, I long for the cold. When it comes, I get tired of splitting wood and I want it to be July." He pulled up in front of the house, stopped the horse, and helped her out of the carriage.

Pete stepped out the door. "I'll take care of Dolly and get her in the barn. Those girls are wound tighter than a top. It'll be a rest to brush down the horse."

Inside, the girls wrapped their arms around Alma's waist.

"You came!" Frances said.

"Of course she did. Papa said she would," Elisbet said. "May I take your cloak, Miss Pickens?"

"Yes, you may. Thank you." Alma slid it from her shoulders and folded it in half before handing it to Elisbet. "There, maybe it won't be quite so hard to carry now."

His girls made him proud. "Thank you, Elisbet."

Elisbet buried her nose in the fabric and came up smiling. "You smell good, like cookies."

"And she has the most beautiful dress." Frances stroked the fabric. "Blue is my favorite color."

"Thank you." Alma's face flushed cranberry red.

Frances snuggled her hand into Alma's and tugged her toward the kitchen. "Come see the table."

Alma looked back at Roy. Was she trying to arch her eyebrow? He couldn't help but grin at her. He figured she didn't know how much his daughters craved a woman's attention. "I'll be right behind you." A place he didn't mind being, because his daughter was right. Alma smelled good.

⁂

Dinner went well. Alma exclaimed over the girls' efforts to make the kitchen "festive," as she called it. He hadn't seen Elisbet's face hold so much joy in months.

"Thank you for tucking them in while I checked on the calf."

"It was fun. I haven't read that princess book in years."

"I can't say the same. It's the same book, or a variation, every night. Think you'll be able to stand that after we're married?" He stood in the parlor. Should he sit next to her on the sofa or in the chair across from her? They'd sat together in the carriage, but that didn't count. Still, it was intimate sitting with a woman without a chaperone. Maybe he'd poke the fire again. "You mentioned a list?"

"I brought it with me." She slid her hand into her dress pocket and pulled out a folded paper. She did that little thing with her eyebrow that was a slight imitation of her father's. On Alma it was downright cute. "You won't toss it in the fire?"

"Maybe after I read it."

"Then sit next to me and I'll read it to you. That will eliminate the chance of its being destroyed." She patted the sofa. "The fire is fine. It's rather warm in here."

Was she bossy? Or practical? Janie never told him what to do. They'd married young, and she thought he could do anything. It had scared him to have someone think he was that capable. He'd let her down in the end. Maybe it would be better to have a wife with her own opinions, used to doing for herself. It would be harder to disappoint her.

He sat by her but not close enough to touch. "Let's hear the demands."

Alma unfolded the paper and held it up. "Isn't it pretty?"

The paper was bordered with tiny birds and flowers. Were those real pieces of ribbons glued to it? Roy nodded.

"I like to paint. I'm learning more about it, and I've been saving for the Oil Painting Outfit Complete with twenty-five colors of paint so I can increase my skills."

Her eyes were wide open and not at all showing any fear that he might disapprove. Not that he would. She'd find out soon enough how little time there would be to paint. "It's good to have something you love to do."

"I do love it. That's why it's on my list."

"Painting?"

"Yes, I want to paint the furniture."

Janie had picked out the furniture he hadn't made for them. "What's wrong with—" Alma dropped her gaze to the floor. He hadn't meant to hurt her, but those were changes he couldn't allow. He'd discuss it with her later. Surely she would understand when he explained what the pieces meant to him. "What else is on that list?"

"First, I want a real wedding at the church, and after it, I want to have cake and punch for our friends. I can make my own wedding dress. Elisbet and Frances should have new ones, too, and shoes, maybe hair ribbons to match."

Roy grasped the paper and slipped it from her hand. "Let me read this." She wanted him to bring her flowers. Where did the woman think he was going to find flowers in November in Illinois? Did she think he had special growing powers that could make them bloom in the middle of winter? It became clear to him there might be a reason she hadn't married. He continued reading. Spend time together every day and. . . "Exchange special gifts at Christmas?" What did that mean?

Chapter 7

Settled on Jewel's sofa, Alma and her friend hunched over a fashion plate in *Godey's Lady's Book*, admiring a dress.

Alma caressed the page. "It's perfect."

"You'll be beautiful. The bottle-green satin will make your eyes look bluer, and with the touches of red on the cuffs and inside the stand-up collar, it's perfect for Christmas."

"I think the cuffs should be red velvet."

"What about the hat?" Jewel wore a cat-grin.

"I'm not wearing a bird, especially a brown one!" Alma put her hands together on top of her head and flapped her fingers as if they were wings. "That would make quite a stir."

"I'm sure the bird is stuffed."

"Doesn't matter. Feathers are fine, but a dead bird is not." Alma frowned. "I have to find a gift for Mr. Gibbons, too." Why had she thought it would be a wonderful idea to make him a special present?

"Shouldn't you call him Roy?"

"I suppose. It feels too soon." And it was. Since she'd agreed to this marriage, her old life had disappeared. Precious objects were packed and stored; furniture had been moved as well. Papa had wasted no time readying to leave. Her body ached with sadness. "Jewel, this is the first time I won't be spending Christmas with Papa."

Jewel slid her arm around Alma's shoulder. "It's going to be fine. You'll be Mrs. Roy Gibbons on Christmas, and you'll have two excited daughters to wake you."

"I don't know what to make him."

"What does he like? What's his favorite color? You could knit a cap."

"I don't know. I wanted to do this because Mama and Papa did, but they were married almost a year before Christmas came." She, of course had to do this the hard way. Meet a man, agree to marry him, and make him a meaningful gift in four weeks.

Jewel's son, Caleb, woke with a scream. "Time for me to go back to being a mother and not a schoolgirl. Why don't you ask around at the store and see if you can discover anything. Mrs. Remik up at the Star Store knows about everyone."

Alma felt light as relief pushed out the sadness. "She does!" She grabbed the *Lady's Godey Book* and held it to her chest. "I'd love to stay and play with Caleb, but I have to go on a spying adventure."

∞

Roy rode up to the front porch and slid down from the saddle. He was worked up about what he'd heard in town. He and Miss Pickens were in need of a serious talk. He rubbed the back of his neck. He'd fallen asleep reading to the girls last night and slept there for a few hours before realizing he wasn't in his own bed.

Alma opened the door with red-rimmed eyes. She'd been crying. His shoulders tensed as he waited for a problem to show up he'd be expected to solve.

"Evening, Mr. Gibbons. Papa isn't home so I can't let you in." She sniffed.

"He's a few minutes behind me. Told me to tell you not to keep me standing outside."

Alma backed away and held the door open. "I always honor my father's requests."

So that's what the crying was about. She still didn't want to marry him. He wasn't sure he wanted to marry her, either, but he'd shaken hands with her father. "It's time you started calling me Roy, don't you think?"

"I suppose so. . .Roy." She closed the door. "I've got dinner about ready to serve for Papa. Would you like some?"

"I came to talk to you, then I need to get home. Pete's with the girls, but I'm feeling bad about having him watch them so I can see you every night." She looked as if she might burst into tears. "Alma, that didn't come out right. Would you be agreeable to a few nights a week instead of—"

"No, I wouldn't. We need to know each other better."

"Is that why you've been asking around town what color shirts I like best and what I buy at the store?"

"Mrs. Remik told you?" Her eyes were wide as a doe's.

"Yes, and when she couldn't understand why you were so interested, I told her we were getting married."

"So now everyone in town knows." Her shoulders sagged as she turned away.

"They'll know soon anyway. I don't see a problem."

"Of course not. Why would you? This is an arrangement between Papa and you. I don't have a choice."

"Is that why you've been crying, Alma?" His heart softened, and he put his hand on her shoulder. He prayed his daughters would never be in this situation. He would do his best from now on to make her feel treasured. Starting with taking her flowers, as soon as he could figure out some way to get some.

"No. It's because. . .I can't get my kitten heads to be round." She rested her hand on his for a moment then brushed it away. "I need to stir. . .something."

Roy scratched his forehead and followed her into the kitchen. He would never understand women, but he knew enough not to ask about the kittens. When it came to females, he'd learned a small problem generally covered a bigger one.

⁓

Alma shivered on the porch step. Elisbet and Frances had rushed past her. "It's early. Why are you here, Roy?"

"I saw your father in town. He said you wouldn't be opposed to watching the girls. I've taken on extra work at the mill and won't be able to meet them after school."

"Papa said to bring them?" How was she to continue packing the house, making her dress, and figuring out what to give Roy for a gift with two little girls running around?

"He thought it'd be a good idea for you all to get to know each other better. He'll watch them while we sit in the parlor after dinner. Doc wants to get to know them, too. Since he'll be their grandfather."

"If he wants to be one, he should stay here in Trenton." She wrapped her arms tight around her waist.

Had he said supper? She needed to cook for all of them every night?

"Then, sweetheart"—he reached out and stroked her cheek—"we might not be getting married." Roy flashed his dimples and then winked.

Sweetheart? Her knees went weak. Her body felt the way it did when she'd been double dosed with Mrs. Winslow's Soothing Syrup—all warm and happy. Did that mean. . .? Could it be that he did care for her?

Chapter 8

Ten inches of snow covered the ground. On his one day off in over a week, Roy ought to be inside doing chores. Instead, once again, he stood on Alma's porch at an odd time of day. Under a heavy blanket, his girls waited in the sleigh. Music-box giggles floated through the air.

Alma squealed with delight at the sight behind him. "Sleigh ride!"

"Would you like to go with us?" Was she bouncing on her toes? "Can you get ready fast? I don't want to undress those two while we wait. It takes too long to put them back together."

"I'll hurry!"

She meant it, because when she appeared less than five minutes later, the twist of hair on the nape of her neck was off center and the yellow ribbon didn't match the skirt he saw hanging from underneath her cloak. The fashionable Miss Pickens had turned into a little girl. She bounded past him, twisting a scarf around her neck. "How long can we ride?"

"Until the first one whines." He helped Alma into the sleigh and slid in next to her. When his arm brushed against hers, sparks he hadn't felt in a long time ignited. He urged the horse forward.

Alma rubbed her muffed hand under her chin. "It's the most beautiful thing, isn't it? Snow? Wouldn't it be perfect if there were bells on the sleigh, Elisbet?"

"Papa! Can we get bells?"

"Bells!" Frances chimed in.

"Please, don't encourage them." Roy glanced at Alma. "What's wrong with your eyebrow?"

"When Papa wants to make a point, he arches his. I can't, not yet. I'm training it." She used her finger to arch it. "Bells are not extravagant, if they make you happy."

Roy pursed his lips then rolled them under. This was not a moment to laugh. "Look, there's a hill and sledders. The snow must be well packed. Anyone want to give it a try?"

A chorus of "I dos" rang from behind him.

He helped everyone from the sleigh and untied the wooden sled he'd brought. "Who's first?"

"Me!" Elisbet said.

"Me!" Frances jumped in front of Elisbet, lost her balance, and toppled in the snow.

"Me!" Alma helped Frances get up. "Let's make snow angels before we go home. That way we won't be as cold and can sled longer."

Alma took him by surprise. He hadn't imagined she'd want to fly down a snowy hill. "I think this sled can hold two, so Franny and I'll go first. Unless, Elisbet, you want to ride with her. She is covered in snow."

Roy lost track of how many runs Alma and the girls, even he, made down the hill. Finally he had to say, "I think it's time to go."

"No, you have to ride with Miss Pickens!" Elisbet insisted.

He started to refuse, but Alma had already climbed on the sled. He settled behind her, the closeness of her, the sweet scent of her hair clutching his heart. Before he let his mind run off the rails, he sent the sled down the hill and into a snow bank. Snow covered her face. Before he could help her up, she giggled then went into a full-throttle laugh, fell backward, and made a snow angel.

"I want to do that again!"

"Maybe next time. I think it's best to get all the red-cheeked women in my life home and warmed up so there aren't any more colds." He couldn't handle another close ride with her. Not until they were married anyway.

He loaded everyone on the sleigh then went to attach the sled to the back. On his way, he noticed a yellow ribbon. He picked it up and slid it into his pocket with a smile. He had his first piece of the gift he'd make Alma.

In the Gibbons' warm kitchen, Alma yanked on Frances's boot until it gave up and released her foot. "Your stockings are wet. Are yours, Elisbet?"

Elisbet nodded.

"Let's find dry clothes for you two before you catch a chill. While we're gone, Roy, could you make some hot chocolate for us?"

"You have to say please." Frances's teeth chattered.

"Please." Alma bent down in front of Frances. "You're right. I should have said that." She stood and took the child's hand. "Shall we?"

Once Alma had the girls in warm clothes, they returned to the kitchen. She'd brought along their brush. "Frances, you're first. Let's get the knots out of your hair." The little girl stood still while her hair was put back in order.

Elisbet took her place. "You hurt less than Papa."

"I've had years of practice unsnarling hair."

"That's true. My hair has never been that long and won't be. Enjoy it, girls, because it's still a few weeks until Christmas."

"And we get Miss Pickens for our mama!" Frances shouted.

"Settle down. The cocoa is ready." He ladled it into cups.

The girls slid into their chairs. Chilled, Alma hesitated. She wanted to sit next to the stove, but that was Roy's seat.

"Sit here," Elisbet demanded, then added, "please."

Roy set cups in front of Frances and Elisbet. "Yes, that's a good spot for you. I'm sure you're cold and wet, too. We should have taken you home first."

"I don't mind. I only did one snow angel, so I wasn't as wet as these two."

Roy placed a cup in front of her. "This will help warm you. Good suggestion, Janie."

If a heart could make a sound when it broke, Alma's would have. Janie. His dead wife's name. She wanted to disappear, be anywhere but Roy Gibbons's kitchen. Her throat closed.

Roy's pale face swam through her watery eyes. "Alma, I'm so sorry. For a moment it felt like we were a family, and I guess that's why I called you Janie. You've filled a vacancy today, and my heart felt whole. Thank you. Can you forgive me, Alma?"

"Is Papa in trouble?" Frances hopped from her chair and was by his side, hot chocolate forgotten.

"No. Everything is fine." Alma offered a forced smile but looked away from Roy. It wasn't good that he took her as a replacement for Janie. He had to understand that before they married. She wasn't sure he would. She loved his children, but Roy never spent time alone with her. He didn't want a wife, he wanted a caretaker. "I am feeling chilled. Would you take me home now?"

∽∾

Roy could have kicked himself. He had called her Janie. Alma had done her best not to let him touch her while he helped her into her cloak. He had to make this better. He could have offered her dry clothes, but that wouldn't do. She wouldn't want to wear the dress of Janie's that he'd kept.

Once in the sleigh, he thought he'd go for distraction. It worked for his daughters. Maybe it would for Alma. "Have you considered what you'd like to bring to the house?"

"My painting equipment, and Papa offered Mama's china. I'd like to bring it." She spoke to the side of the

70

sleigh instead of turning his way.

"We'll probably find a place to store things in the barn. Janie's china is still serviceable, and I'm not sure where we'd put your paints."

"As you wish."

This wasn't going well. He'd planned to kiss her when he took her home, but now? He'd best wait.

Chapter 9

Something roused Roy. Had Frances cried out? He pushed against the chair arms and rose. He didn't hear her now.

He was heartsick about calling Alma the wrong name. Even thought of getting Pete to watch the girls so he could go talk to her. Get her to understand he liked having her in his kitchen. Instead, after getting the girls down for the night, he had sat down to rest and had drifted off.

A knock sounded. "Gibbons!"

Roy jerked open the door. "Dr. Pickens. Is Alma all right?"

"No, she is not." Dr. Pickens marched past him. "I thought you were a decent man." He paced the room. "I'm giving you my most valuable possession because I thought you were worthy. It seems I'm wrong."

"Doc, can I—"

"No sir, you cannot. I have a lot to say. My little girl has been in her room since you brought her home. She's crying, and I can't make her stop." He faced Roy.

"Do you know how that feels?"

Not sure if he was allowed to speak, Roy just nodded.

"I know you do, because you've been raising those girls alone. That's why this match is a good one. You need each other, but you can't be calling my Alma by your wife's name." He lowered himself into a chair. "Now what is your explanation?"

Roy sat across from the doctor, dipped his head, and held his forehead with his hands. "It slipped out. Everything felt normal, like we were a family again. I tried to tell her that."

"She doesn't expect you to quit loving Janie. She knows what it's like to lose someone you love, but son, you have to do what your vows said."

What vows? He and Alma hadn't said any yet. Confused, Roy straightened his back and gaped at him.

"Remember the part that says, 'until death do us part'? You have to release Janie and let Alma move into your heart. She needs the bigger space now. Show her you care enough to remember her name. All this coming over to our house in the evening is nice, but it's not enough. Alma was right. You need to court her, so you mean it when you say those vows to her. You better repair this mess right away. Otherwise, you might as well hire a woman to come help in this house."

"I took her sledding."

"With your children."

"She didn't mind." He stopped from squirming like a ten-year-old caught with his hand in the cookie jar. Why had he thought this would be easy? Alma didn't know him, and he shouldn't expect her to.

"Take her out alone. There's always a bonfire on the weekend down by the pond at Sauer's place. Bring her candy. Take her ice skating. Hold her hand. Stare into her eyes. Make her feel like she's the only one in the world. Janie agreed to marry you, so you must know how to court a woman. Do you remember?"

Yes, he did, and the memory hurt. Could he do those things with Alma?

❧

Alma's heart wasn't in making Roy's gift. She'd failed to find out more about him. She knew he cared about his family, but beyond that, she hadn't even discovered his favorite color. She strolled the store aisle searching for something to use to craft an ornament.

She fingered silk ribbons. Elisbet and Frances would like these. They were easy to buy for, not like their father. If God would send her an idea of what to make, something Roy would save and treasure, she'd be grateful.

The door opened and the sunlight struck something, sending a rainbow through the room. She picked up her pace, and there it was. A beautiful, clear, glass teardrop ornament. The perfect size for painting. She purchased it along with the ribbons and hurried home as the sun set.

She slowed her step. Roy sat on the porch rail waiting for her.

"I heard there was a bonfire tonight. I'd like to take you, just you, if you'll go with me," he asked.

Thrilled, Alma ran upstairs and put away her purchases, found warm clothes, and met him at the door. Minutes later they were at Sauer's pond sitting by a bonfire and lacing on their skates. He'd said little to her on the ride and even now remained quiet. Maybe it was time for her to let go of her anger and give him an opportunity to start over.

She could either continue to be furious or take it as a compliment that Roy was comfortable with her. The fire crackled and popped behind her. "Are we going to be like the wild young ones and take a chance on the ice, or stay by the fire like our elders?"

Roy's eyes flashed in the firelight. Then he took her hand. "I'm not feeling like an elder, so let's be young, but not wild. Unless you want to be?"

Was that uncertainty, or fear in his voice? "Not up to falling and spinning on the ice tonight?"

"Not when I have to be a father in the morning. If I could lie around in bed like you all day, counting the flowers on the wallpaper, then I might."

She playfully slapped his arm. "I have never lain in bed all day."

"What do you do with your days?"

"Lots of things. Paint, feed the chickens, gather feathers for projects." Alma waved at her friend Katie and her brother as they swished by. "Make dinner for Papa."

"Feathers? What do you do with them?"

"I'm working on a dye to color them or sometimes I try to paint them." Her foot slipped. "Oh!"

Roy caught her, brought her upright, and steadied her. "You paint them and then what?"

"I haven't found the best application for them, yet. They may have something to do with your special Christmas gift." She gave her best mystery-smile and skated away. Feathers. Perhaps she could find some way to adhere them to his gift.

Roy circled her then slipped in next to her, taking her hand. "Want to play a game?"

She attempted the eyebrow arch and felt it go a tiny

bit higher. "What kind?"

"A getting-to-know-you game. I'll give you two choices and you guess which one I like. Then you get a turn."

"I'm first." She dropped his hand, skated ahead and did a spin, and returned with a question. "Christmas or Fourth of July?

"You like Christmas, because we'll be married by then."

"I do like it best, but not because we'll be married. I love the nativity story and that's when Jesus was born."

"I like that you'll be my wife and you get to be there when the girls jump out of bed and their eyes are wide with excitement. I can't wait for you to see that."

The thin layer of ice around her heart began to drip. He did want to marry her. He'd said that first before anything else. She should apologize for leaving in a huff the other day." Roy pulled her tight to him as they rounded the end of the frozen pond. "Working in the field or with wood?"

"I think"—she tilted her head and studied his face—"the field, because it provides for your family."

"Both do, and while I'm grateful, the fields don't provide much enjoyment. I like making things out of wood."

"So my gift is made of wood?" She giggled.

"Still a secret. You might be getting nothing more than a splinter."

"Orange or black?"

"Odd choices for favorite colors. Orange?"

"Black. I like black cats." A small group of boys began to race on the ice, whizzing past at dizzying speeds. The bonfire looked appealing.

"Cats make me sneeze. Do you think I'd rather eat pork chops or roast and potatoes?"

"Pork chops."

"Roast, because the next day I can have a delicious sandwich. I haven't had a good roast since Janie—"

A few boys raced past. One tripped, and his arms went in wild circles as he attempted to stay on his feet. He fell, sliding in their direction. Alma squealed.

Roy whipped Alma away from the sharp blades before they reached her. She ought to be grateful, but all she remembered was hearing the name Janie—again.

⟡

In the barn, Roy caressed a piece of wood. He had to prove to Alma he cared. He'd seen the look on her face when he'd mentioned Janie again. If he wanted, and he did, to build a life with her, he needed to start with a good foundation.

He hadn't lied to her when he'd said she'd get a splinter for Christmas, because she surely would. But it wasn't her only gift. He had the special one finished, ready for Christmas.

Chapter 10

"Remember you can't tell your father about this." Alma tied Frances's apron and then checked to make sure Elisbet was well covered.

Before the girls arrived, Alma had covered the kitchen table with last week's *Trenton Gazette* to protect it from the red and green paint she'd mixed for them to use.

"We won't." Elisbet shoved her fists under her chin and squealed. "We keep secrets, don't we, Franny?"

"Yeth." Franny gave a missing-tooth grin. Her front tooth had fallen out last week, making her even more adorable.

Alma was unsure about these two. They tended to tell their father about their day the moment they saw him. "Let's sit at the kitchen table. Be careful—" They were in their chairs, feet kicking against the bottom rungs before she finished her sentence. "Not to knock over the paint."

"What are we painting?" Elisbet turned in her chair. "I don't see anything worth keeping a secret."

"I get the green!" Frances shouted.

"Frances, no yelling. There is enough of both colors. Turn back around, Elisbet. What we are painting is in my apron pocket."

The room grew quiet as Alma reached into her pocket and withdrew the ornament wrapped in brown paper. "This is it." She sat between them, set the package on the table, and lifted an edge of the paper, gently unwinding it. "It's made of glass. We have to be careful."

Alma held the ornament up for them to see. "We are going to paint our names on it. What do you think?"

No response. No excitement. No anything. She looked at each girl. No smiles. "What's wrong?"

"Franny can't write her name."

"I'll help her. Would that be okay, Frances?"

"Yeth. Can we paint the paper, too?"

"That's a good idea. While Elisbet paints her name on the ornament, you can work on half of the wrapping paper. Then we can switch."

The girls worked with occasional giggles, and Alma had to wipe paint from the ends of their hair a few times.

"Finished!" Frances glowed. "All my letterth are on there."

Including an adorable fingerprint. Alma didn't know if Roy would cherish it, but she would.

"Can we put your name and Papa's on it?" Elisbet asked. "Because Papa said we're going to be a family. So, can we?"

Alma's heart swelled with love. "Yes, and we'll hang it on our tree every year."

She finished the last stroke on Roy's *y*. The back door swung open. Her father rushed in, breathless. "The church is on fire. The wedding's canceled. Roy's on his way. Meet him at the front door, and I'll hide this."

∽

"We are getting married." Roy shivered in the cold air. The water on his pants had turned to ice. "Can I come in?"

"Yes, of course. You're wet. Go in the parlor where it's warm. I'll get hot chocolate for you, to chase the chill."

"I want—need you to come with me." He grasped her hand and pulled her along with him. Standing with his back to the fire, willing his teeth not to chatter, he drew her close and kissed her. "Alma Gail Pickens will you marry me?"

"I don't under—"

"Just answer the question."

"Yes."

Her face crinkled, and her eyebrow arched. Did she realize it? He wanted to laugh and then shout, "I love Alma Pickens!"

"Roy?" Her questioning eyes begged for more.

He kissed her again, feeling the heat thaw his lips. "I saw the church in flames, and I knew the wedding would be called off. Then I realized, if this had happened tomorrow while we were there, I might have lost you, and I haven't told you how I feel. That I love the way you make every activity fun, the way you practice your eyebrow arch, and the way you make me feel like more than a father. You've given me my life back, and I never even proposed to you. You deserve that. So I'll ask you again, Alma, would you marry me? Could you love me the rest of our lives?"

"Yes! I love you, too. But how will we get married? The girls are counting on having a mother on Christmas morning."

"Don't worry. I have a plan. If you keep Elisbet and Frances tonight, I promise to make tomorrow a special memory, even without the church." He tipped her head and kissed her again.

"Are you going to kiss me a lot when we're married?"

"Yes, I am."

"I'm glad. I didn't know I'd like it so much." Her face flushed a bright red. "I should get you something to drink, to warm you."

"I don't need anything. You've thawed my frozen bones, sweetheart."

∞

Alma waited in Roy's bedroom, trying hard not to think that it would be her bedroom, too, tonight. Her father had covered her eyes when they entered the house, and the girls led her in so she couldn't see the decorations. Her hands shook. How she wished Mama was here. Jewel had explained a few things to her, with a scarlet face. Her father had come to her room last night to discuss with her the duties of a wife. Horrified, she'd sent him away.

She'd helped Elisbet and Frances into their red velvet dresses and tied bows in their hair. Their faces were blinding with joy as they scooted from the room. Jewel had helped her put on her dress. The satin, soft as a kitten, slid over her head. She rubbed the red velvet cuff between her fingers. It was perfect. Even more so, she knew she would honor her mother and father by marrying Roy.

It was almost time. Soon she'd be Mrs. Roy Gibbons.

Her stomach twirled. She promised God she would be the best wife and mother possible. The door opened, and her father stepped inside, beaming.

He held out his arm. "You're beautiful, Little Bit. So much like your mother. Are you ready?"

Alma took his elbow and they strolled past the dining room. Roy had placed Mama's embroidered tablecloth under heaping platters of bread and meat. China dishes and. . .were those Mama's cups? They were. Her eyes watered. It felt right, almost as if Mama were here, smiling. It was beautiful, festive.

But the parlor took her breath away. Candles in crystal holders ambled across the mantel, sending warm, dancing lights across the room. A music box played in the background, and Roy waited for her by the fire with the preacher. He'd kept his promise. He'd given her a wedding to remember.

∞

The bedroom door creaked. Alma started. She heard giggles and opened her eyes.

"Good morning, Mrs. Gibbons." Roy stood inside the door, holding tight to his daughters' shoulders. "They have something to say." He let go, and blond hair flew as Elisbet and Frances ran and jumped on the bed.

Elisbet tapped Frances's shoulder. "One, two, three."

"Merry Christmas, Mama!" Alma treasured the unison of the sweet voices.

"Come on, girls, let's let your mama get dressed and meet us in the parlor."

Alma smiled at her new husband with gratitude.

The girls waited by the tree, pointing out decorations they liked. They asked questions about how the tree got into the house without them knowing, and when could they open presents. They were elated at the ribbons from Alma and the gifts from Roy.

"Mrs. Gibbons? I believe you are to give me a special gift?"

Alma giggled. "It's here." She hopped to her feet and brought out a package.

"We painted the paper!" Frances shouted. "And we—"

"Hush, Franny." Elisbet covered Frances's mouth. "You're giving it away. Open it, Papa!"

"Remove your hand from your sister's mouth, please." Roy unwrapped the ornament and, if possible, the dimples in his cheeks grew deeper as he smiled.

"Do you like it?" Alma thought so, but wanted to hear him say it.

"I do. I see our names and one fingerprint. The feather is a nice touch. That's from you, Alma?"

"Yes, and the fingerprint is from Frances. I thought it was special."

"It is, and we will cherish this. One day, this will hang on your tree, Frances."

Elisbet frowned. "Why does she get to have it?"

"Just wait." Roy drew a package from his pocket. "Here is my gift, Alma."

She opened the paper. Inside was an ornament made of blond braided hair shaped into a heart and glued to a small piece of wood. A yellow ribbon twisted with a piece of a black string tie wove through a hole and tied to use as a hanger. "Is this my ribbon?"

"And my tie. I wanted this gift to represent our family."

"I love it." Alma pressed it to her heart. "Elisbet, someday this will be yours."

∞

Later, Roy slipped a kiss on Alma's neck. "Remember when I said you were going to get a splinter for Christmas?"

"But I didn't. You sanded the wood smoothly."

"I made you something else." Roy's heart beat fast, ready to explode.

Alma's face filled with excitement.

"Come to the barn with me." Once they were

inside he led her to a stall and yanked off the tattered quilt covering the blanket chest he'd built. "I wanted to start this marriage off with a piece of furniture we both made. I've done my part. Now it's up to you to paint it any way you like."

Alma dropped to her knees. She ran her hand across the daises he'd carved on the front panel. "Daisies."

"To get you through the winter until I can bring you real ones."

"It's so beautiful." She opened the lid and gasped. "The Oil Painting Outfit Complete!" She jumped up and wrapped her arms around him. "I love you, Roy Gibbons."

"I love you, too." She fit him more perfectly than he ever could have imagined. God had replaced his pain and loss with Alma, who taught him true love could come more than once in a lifetime.

About the Author

Diana Lesire Brandmeyer writes historical and contemporary romances. She is the author of *Mind of Her Own*, *A Bride's Dilemma in Friendship, Tennessee* and *We're Not Blended, We're Pureed: A Survivor's Guide to Blended Families*. Once widowed and now remarried, she writes with humor and experience on the difficulty of joining two families, be it fictional or real life.

Please visit her webpage, www.dianabrandmeyer.com

Bigger. Better. Together.
Stories of love, blending and bonding.

The Christmas Tree Bride

By Susan Page Davis

Chapter 1

Stage Stop along the Oregon Trail
Wyoming 1867

Polly Winfield dashed about the dining room, setting up. On days the stage came through, she and her mother always prepared to serve a full table. The passengers would eat quickly, reboard the stagecoach, and hurry away toward the next station.

Polly didn't mind the hectic mornings on Wednesdays. The stage was heading west, and that meant Jacob Tierney would be driving it. He would blow the brass horn to announce their arrival and canter the horses the last few hundred yards, to put on a good show. After the passengers gulped down Ma's stew and biscuits and pie, they would go on, but Jacob would stay.

The young man had recently landed the job as replacement driver for old Norm Hatfield, who had been injured in a driving mishap when his team was spooked by lightning and ran away with the stage. If Norm recovered, or if the division agent hired another permanent driver, Jacob wouldn't come by the Winfield Station anymore. But that wouldn't happen for a while. At least, Polly hoped not. She liked Jacob enormously, and he had told her he expected to drive the route another three or four weeks, until the line stopped operation for the winter.

The best part of the arrangement was that Jacob stayed at the Winfields' home station from Wednesday until Saturday, when the stage returned, heading east. The driver on that run, Harry Smith, would stay there from Saturday until Jacob returned the following Wednesday. They each had a run of 120 miles or so, covering six stations. On their days between runs, the drivers could do whatever they pleased. If Polly had anything to say about it, Jacob would be pleased to further their acquaintance.

Ma bustled through the kitchen doorway carrying two covered baskets. "They'll be here any minute. Set these out and fill the water pitchers."

Polly took the baskets and set them on the table, enjoying the fresh scent of baking. The passengers always raved about Ma's flaky biscuits. Polly had heard more than once that the Winfield Station had the best food of any along the line from Fort Laramie to Salt Lake City.

She filled the pitchers with water straight from the well and made sure each place setting was perfect. Ma would serve the stew in shallow ironstone soup plates, and the diners could set their biscuits on the broad edge.

The faint call of Jacob's horn reached her. The stage was coming down the slope from the bluffs. She longed to run outside and watch him guide the team in, but Ma would have a fit if she disappeared now. Their job was to get the meal on the table and make sure every passenger was satisfied, while Pa collected the price of dinner and the tenders swapped the tired horses for a fresh team.

Jacob's duties ended when the last passenger stepped down from the coach. He'd give Pa and Harry any news he'd picked up along the way and then mosey out back to use the necessary and wash up. When the passengers were done eating and were scrambling back into the coach, he would stroll into the dining room and grin at Polly and say, "What's to eat?"

Polly smiled as the first passenger came through the door. The next quarter hour would be hectic, but so worth the fuss. Her mother earned nearly as much with her cooking as Pa earned for running the station.

Eight men paid up and came to the table today. Ma

was smiling, and Polly knew she was adding up the money in her head. The coaches had been full every week in the summer and autumn, but now cold weather was setting in, and sometimes Jacob had only one or two riders. People hated riding the stage in freezing weather.

Polly filled coffee cups, brought more biscuits, and distributed slices of apple pie. She glanced out the window once. The tenders were guiding the fresh team into place.

"Got more coffee, miss?" one of the diners asked, and Polly hurried to get it.

A moment later, Harry poked his head in the doorway and yelled, "All aboard!"

Men grabbed one last bite of their dessert or a final swallow of coffee and headed out to the yard.

And there he was, leaning against the doorjamb, grinning, his whip coiled in his hand.

"What's to eat, Polly?" he asked.

She laughed. "You know we always have beef stew on Wednesday."

He stepped forward and took a seat at the end of the long table. "Did you save me any biscuits?"

"I always do." Polly whisked away the dirty dishes from the table in front of him and hurried to the kitchen. "Jacob's ready to eat."

"What about the shotgun messenger?" Ma asked. "Is Billy Clyde with him?"

"Haven't seen him yet," Polly said.

Ma ladled a generous serving of stew into a soup plate. "I'm saving enough for him. Didn't expect so many passengers today, though. They nearly cleaned me out."

Polly carried the stew and a basket of warm biscuits into the dining room.

"Where's Billy Clyde?" she asked Jacob.

"Out yonder, jawing with your pappy." Jacob's eyes lit up when she put the plate of stew before him. "I've been dreaming of this stew all week."

"Naw, he ain't," Billy Clyde said from the doorway. "Miss Polly, he's been dreamin' 'bout you."

Polly laughed and felt her cheeks warm. "Hush you, Billy Clyde." The shotgun rider had been with the line since it opened, and stayed with it when Wells Fargo bought out the previous owners. He was nearly Pa's age, lean and lithe. His beard showed some gray, and he limped from a wound he'd received courtesy of a road agent three years back.

Billy Clyde always teased Polly—and any other female in sight—but they said he'd never seriously courted a woman. He complained a lot, especially in bad weather when his leg ached, but he'd become a fixture at Winfield Station, and he was Pa's closest friend.

Ma came in from the kitchen carrying a soup plate for Billy Clyde and two mugs.

"There you are." She smiled at Billy Clyde.

"Couldn't stay away," he replied.

Polly began to stack the passengers' dishes while Ma poured coffee and lingered to banter with Billy Clyde. Jacob tucked into his meal and seemed disinclined to talk until his belly was filled.

Pa had warned Polly when they first moved here last year to keep away from the men, but she was sure he mostly meant the tenders. They were rough-hewn and loud, and they cursed and played poker in the bunkroom that was part of the barn. Billy Clyde might be unpolished, and he might even join the poker game now and then, but he was always polite, and Pa seemed confident that his women were safe around him.

Jacob was altogether different, quieter and more courteous than the others. When a chore needed doing, he offered to help, whether it was sweeping the dining room or toting firewood. He never gambled with the other men. Last week, Polly heard Billy Clyde confide to Pa, "Young Tierney won't even go near the saloon at the fort. And I offered to buy." Maybe Billy Clyde considered that unmanly, but it was music to Polly's ears.

She hummed a hymn as she washed the dishes. From the dining room, the men's cheerful voices reached her. Wednesday was Polly's favorite day of the week, hands down.

Pa came in, carrying two coffee mugs. "New pot ready?"

"Should be." Polly resumed her humming as she scrubbed the empty stew pot.

"Oh, there's something for you in the mail, Polly."

"For me?"

"Yes—from your friend Ava."

Polly dried her hands on her apron and dashed into the dining room. The small pile of mail lay on the table by Pa's empty chair. Beneath two envelopes he had opened, she found a colorful square postal card. She gasped and picked it up.

"Pretty, isn't it?" Jacob said.

Polly nodded. "It's a Christmas tree."

"I've never seen one," Billy Clyde said.

The pictured evergreen was decked in glass ornaments and small candles, the way the Germans trimmed their trees. Polly turned the card over and smiled at the sight of Ava's handwriting.

Miss you. Hope you have a good Christmas. We are going to my grandmother Neal's. Love, Ava

Her father came in from the kitchen carrying the mugs, now filled with steaming coffee.

"Pa, can we have a Christmas tree this year?" Polly asked.

"What do you want with that foolishness?" Pa asked, but his tone wasn't sharp.

"Oh, come on, Pa. We always had one back home."

Pa set one mug in front of Billy Clyde and the other before Jacob and sat down. "Polly, this is home now. And trees are hard to come by in Wyoming. I'm a busy man, and I don't have time to traipse around looking for a Christmas tree."

Polly sighed and turned the card over to gaze at the beautiful tree. The artist had drawn it in a background of fluffy snow, but she doubted anyone would really decorate a tree outdoors like that. Still, it was pretty, and a saucy red bird perched on the highest branch, more beautiful than the hand-blown ornaments.

"Polly," her mother called from the kitchen.

She tucked the card into the pocket of her dress and hurried back to her chores.

A few minutes later, her father poked his head in the doorway. "The men are done eating. You can clear the table."

Polly turned partway around and caught his eye. "Are you sure we can't find a tree somewhere, Pa?"

He sighed. "I told you, I don't have time. But the men don't have much to do for the next couple of days. Why don't you ask them to get you one?"

Pa left the kitchen, but Polly didn't go back to humming. Was a Christmas tree such a hard thing to find out here? Of course, they had fewer trees than back in New England. But still. . .

She missed a lot of things about Massachusetts, and no matter what Pa said, she still thought of it as home.

On her arrival at the stage stop with her mother a year and a half ago, Polly was excited by the newness of everything. She had immediately been pressed into service, but she didn't mind. She was contributing to the family's income.

She kept very active in the summer and autumn. When she wasn't needed to prepare meals, serve, do dishes, or perform other chores, she explored the rolling grasslands around their new home. She loved the wildflowers and her frequent sightings of birds, prairie dogs, coyotes, and now and then a herd of antelope.

But the birds and flowers here looked different, and there were no neat little villages or close neighbors. She missed her friends, especially Ava. She missed the trees, too. No spreading maples out here, no hardy oaks or waving birches.

And she had not been prepared for the bleak winter of the prairie.

Last winter she had keenly felt the isolation of the station. She and Ma had stitched a quilt, curtains, and several items of clothing for the family. The stagecoaches couldn't get through for nearly three months, and in all that time they'd had only one another to talk to, besides an occasional hardy trapper who ventured out on snowshoes, one cavalry detail, and a couple of small bands of Shoshone who stopped in, hoping to trade.

The Indians had frightened Polly a little, but they seemed friendly enough. Pa had allowed Polly to trade a pair of outgrown shoes for a small beaded pouch that now housed her embroidery needle and silk thread. The items for her fancywork had been a gift from her grandmother one Christmas, and the thought lowered Polly's spirits even further. No more Christmas gifts under the tree. No more Christmas Day visits to Grandpa and Grandma Winfield's house for a huge turkey dinner with her aunts and uncles and cousins.

As she tossed the dishwater out the back door, Polly noticed how dark the sky was. Maybe they would have snow before nightfall. The air was certainly cold enough.

She determined to ask Jacob if he would find a tree for her. They may not have relatives to share the holiday with, and there may be no ornaments for the tree, but a Christmas tree would fill a small piece of the gap in her heart.

Chapter 2

Jacob was reading in the room he shared with Billy Clyde when someone knocked firmly on the door. He laid aside his book and went to answer it. Polly stood under the overhanging eaves at the back of the house, smiling at him with her dimples showing in her cheeks.

"Hello," Jacob said.

"Hello, yourself. Ma thinks we should do laundry since it's warm today. Got anything you want washed?"

"That's very kind of you. Hold on." Hastily, Jacob gathered up a few things. He hadn't put on his long johns this morning, so he rolled them up in his dirtiest shirt, along with a pair of socks. He was glad he had spread up his bunk earlier, as Polly stood in the doorway, gazing unabashedly around the room. Billy Clyde's bunk was a heap of quilts and linen, and Jacob hoped Polly wouldn't take offense.

"Here you go." He passed her the bundle, a wave of heat passing over him as he realized she'd be seeing his longies. "Uh, what about Billy Clyde?"

"I asked him before he and Pa went hunting, and he

said he didn't need anything washed." Polly wrinkled her nose as if she disagreed strongly with Billy Clyde on what constituted "clean enough."

"Well, thanks."

Polly looked up at him suddenly and grinned. "Say, would you get me a Christmas tree?"

Jacob couldn't have been more surprised if the tenders had brought a team of bison out of the barn for his next run.

"A Christmas tree?"

"Yes. Pa says he's too busy to look for one, but he said I could ask you fellows if you'd have time."

"Well, now, I'd have to think on where I could find one." Jacob scratched his chin.

"I know it'd be a ways. Pa has to go miles and miles to find any firewood." Polly's blue eyes held a wistful, faraway look.

"Means a lot to you, does it?" Jacob asked.

She smiled as though a little embarrassed. "More than I realized. It's pretty out here, but it's so different."

"I guess you had a lot of forests where you came from."

She nodded. "My friend Ava and I used to hang our skates around our necks and walk to the pond."

"Ice skates? I never had any," Jacob said. "It hardly

froze for a minute down in Arkansas."

"You poor thing. I loved skating on the pond. It was grand fun. Sometimes Pa would build a bonfire on the bank at dusk, and everyone would come from miles around to join in the party. It was almost like going to a dance."

"Sounds like a good time. But what's all that got to do with trees?"

Polly chuckled ruefully. "I thought of it when you asked me about the forest. To get to the pond, we'd pass through a big pine grove, where it was all shadowy and spooky some days. But in summer, it was cool and shady in there."

"Which did you like best?"

"Summer, I guess, but winter wasn't so bad. Here, it's lonesome. Everything's dead as far as you can see. The line shuts down. Nobody comes to visit. And last Christmas, we didn't even have a tree. It just seemed wrong, and sort of. . .depressing."

She looked lost then, and more than anything, Jacob wanted to bring the merry smile back to her face. He squared his shoulders. "There's some scrub pines in the hills between here and Fort Laramie. I'll see what I can do on my next run."

Her whole face lit up, and she clutched the bundle

of laundry tighter. "Thank you ever so much!"

"It'd be an honor. That is, if I can find one."

"We always had a balsam fir in Massachusetts." Her eyes took on that yearning look again. "We had a few ornaments—not many. I'm not even sure Ma brought them along. But we'd string popcorn and cranberries and cut stars and snowflakes out of paper. And when it was all trimmed, it looked grand."

"Well, I don't know as I can find a fir tree. Would a pine or a cedar do, if I can't?"

Polly laid a hand on his sleeve, and Jacob felt her warmth through the flannel. "At this point, I'll take any kind of an evergreen. Just a small one—I don't want it scraping the ceiling in the parlor, but maybe six feet or so. Of course, I don't want you to spend days and days looking for one, but it would mean so much to me."

Jacob smiled and nodded, feeling kind of like his insides had turned to pudding. Like his smile was crooked, and maybe his thinking was, too. Polly didn't have the dignified beauty of a fairy princess, but she was pretty, and she sure did make him see that pond in the woods where she skated, and the tree festooned with popcorn garlands. If he could keep that look on her face for a few days by bringing her a scraggly little pine tree, it would certainly be worthwhile. Somehow, the thought of making her happy made him happy.

∞

That evening, Jacob enjoyed dinner with the family, Billy Clyde, and the tenders. Mrs. Winfield outdid herself with fried chicken, potatoes, and gravy. She'd cooked up a squash and some beets, too. Jacob didn't see too many fresh vegetables this time of year. The Winfields must have a well-stocked root cellar. And the cake that came after—now, that was something. Mrs. Winfield let on that Polly had made it. Polly blushed and giggled and thanked the men prettily for their compliments. Jacob thought that was fine—that a girl who worked hard and showed winsome ways could cook to boot.

The tenders headed out for the barn when the cake and coffee were gone, and Billy Clyde followed shortly after. Mr. Winfield pushed back his chair and said he thought he'd go and check the stock.

"Those Mormon fellows that came through from Fort Bridger said there's a band of Arapahoe on the move. Seems late for them to migrate to their winter camp. I want to make sure they don't take a fancy to any of our horses or mules."

"Can I help you, sir?" Jacob asked.

"Maybe so. I think I'll run them inside for the

108

night. The boys won't like it. They'll have to clean out the barn in the morning."

"That's better than losing your teams," Jacob said.

When Jacob came back to the house twenty minutes later, Polly was elbow-deep in dishwater, and her mother was putting away the supper things.

"Anything I can help with, ma'am?" he asked from the kitchen doorway.

"Oh, thank you, Jacob," Mrs. Winfield replied with a smile. "I think we have it in hand. Everything all right in the barn?"

"Yes ma'am. All the horses and mules are inside now. Well, goodnight."

Polly looked at him over her shoulder with that saucy little dimpled smile. "Goodnight!"

Oh, she was pretty all right.

∽∾

Two wagons full of supplies for the winter arrived Friday, and Jacob and Billie Clyde helped Pa and the tenders unload it. They lugged sacks of feed to the barn and boxes to the lean-to behind the kitchen.

Polly helped her mother bake bread and pies for the stagecoach trade that would come on Saturday, and she and Jacob smiled at each other every time he passed through the kitchen with a load.

"Guess the rest will have to go in the barn," Pa said after they'd made about a dozen trips each.

"I just toted two buckets of axle grease in," Jacob said, "but I guess it should go to the barn."

"Land, yes. Anything that's for the stagecoach or the livestock, put out there," Pa said. "Just foodstuffs and coal in the lean-to."

"Yes sir." Jacob looked a little embarrassed that he had made such a mistake. He went into the lean-to and returned with two five-gallon buckets.

"Oh, Jacob, when you're finished, I've got your clean clothes for you," Polly called after him.

"Thank you kindly." His face was a dull red as he went out.

"Now, Polly," Ma said gently, "men don't like to think of ladies handling their unmentionables. Best let me give him his things when he comes back."

"All right." Polly went back to rolling out piecrust. How was she supposed to know these things if no one told her?

Jacob and Billy Clyde were invited to spend a leisurely evening with the family. Pa played checkers with the other two men in turns, but neither of them could beat him. Polly sat demurely on the settee beside her mother in the cozy parlor, embroidering a special center square for her next quilt, while Ma knitted. With a coal fire in the potbellied stove, the room stayed warm, though outside the wind buffeted the station.

"I won't wonder if we get snow soon," Ma said.

"Maybe you boys will get snowed in here," Pa added.

"It'd have to be a lot of snow to do that." Billy Clyde moved his checkers with a *click-click-click*. "There! King me!"

Pa chuckled. "Pratt sent word with the supply wagons that they'll keep the stages running as long as they possibly can."

"I don't fancy getting stuck in a snowdrift with a stage full of drummers," Billy Clyde said.

"What about you, Jacob?" Pa asked. "Do you like driving in snow?"

"I don't mind, so long as I've got warm gloves and a good wool hat." Jacob stacked up the checkers Pa had already taken from Billy Clyde. "I hope we can keep on for a couple more weeks at least."

"Wanting to draw your full pay for the month, hey?" Billy Clyde said.

Jacob nodded. "This position's just temporary for me. If I'm going to be out of a job soon, I'd like to have enough to buy a good saddle horse, so's I can set out and find another place to work."

Polly's spirits plummeted. She had hoped Jacob would stay in the area. If he was leaving soon for parts unknown, the hopes she had nourished were nothing but childish dreams.

She tried not to look at Jacob too often, but the next time she glanced his way, their gazes caught and he smiled at her. The shock of warmth that washed over her almost knocked her off the settee.

After an hour or so of checkers, fancywork, and placid conversation, Ma put aside her knitting and stood. "Would you fellows like some gingerbread before you go to bed?"

Polly stuck her needle through the material of her quilt square and tucked it into her workbag while her mother took beverage orders. She hurried to the kitchen to help.

"I left a jug of milk in the lean-to," Ma said. "Will you get that?"

Polly retrieved it and poured a cup for Jacob and one for herself. Ma had poured out mugs of coffee and opened the pie safe. She set the pan of gingerbread on the table.

"You cut that, and I'll whip some cream."

Polly cut generous squares of the fragrant

gingerbread for each of the men and more modest ones for herself and Ma. She took the men's beverages into the parlor on a tray. Pa was engrossed in his checker strategy, but Jacob smiled up at her as he took his milk.

"Thanks, Polly."

"Makes me hate to leave this station." Billy Clyde raised his cup and blew on the surface of his steaming coffee. "Why, if I had my druthers, I'd stay here all week."

"You could sign on as a tender," Pa said grimly. "We'll likely lose Roberts soon." He'd been having some trouble with the men lately, getting them to stick to their tasks of keeping the harness in good shape and the horses immaculately groomed. Polly knew that the stocky man called Roberts wasn't happy at the prospect of getting stranded here for the winter and was talking about quitting.

Billy Clyde snorted a laugh. "As if I'd take less pay to sleep in the barn and never get to town. Although Miz Winfield's vittles would be a benefit to consider."

"You'd get so fat and lazy, come spring you wouldn't be able to roll out of your bunk to harness a team," Pa said.

Polly smiled at that. Billy Clyde was so thin, she doubted he would ever be fat, even if he spent a whole winter eating Ma's cooking and getting no exercise.

"It might be nice to have friends here at Christmas," Ma said.

"Was you all alone last year?" Billy Clyde asked.

"You should know," Pa said, looking over the checkerboard. "You left with the tenders, a week before Christmas, and then the snow came. I didn't mind. It was restful. But I began to think Bertha and Polly would go a mite crazy."

Ma smiled. "We three had to celebrate Christmas and New Year's alone, and didn't see a soul for most of January either. Finally a bunch of troopers came through, breaking trail."

"I wish we could go back East for Christmas," Polly said. Pa frowned at her, and she added, "Oh, I don't mean to stay. The holidays just don't seem the same without the decorations and the carols and our loved ones all around us."

"I'll try to bring you that tree you hanker for," Jacob said.

"Oh, so this is the one you've drawn into your scheme." Pa shook his head.

"I don't mind." Jacob looked at Polly, as if for support.

"He said he might have time, Pa, and you did

say I could ask."

"Yes, I did."

"Better you than me," Billy Clyde said, reaching to move one of his checkers.

They said no more about the tree or Christmas, and Polly hoped she hadn't embarrassed Jacob too badly by enlisting his help.

While Ma resumed her knitting, Jacob said quietly, "That was mighty fine gingerbread, Mrs. Winfield."

"Thank you, Jacob. Now, tell us where you're from and how long you expect to be driving this run."

"I'm from Arkansas originally, ma'am, but I came out here from Independence. The division agent hired me just temporary."

"He ought to keep you on," Billy Clyde said. "You're doing all right driving."

"Thanks. I've always wanted to drive stage. I was driving a freight wagon in Independence, but that's not the same."

Billy Clyde snorted. "Not hardly."

"I do need the job badly. I don't know where I'll go when they turn me loose."

"Well, don't waste time on your run looking for a tree for my daughter," Pa said.

"He can't do that," Billie Clyde assured him. "Can't

stop the stage unless it's an emergency."

"Yeah, I'd lose my place for sure if I did that." Jacob looked over at Polly and smiled. "Don't you worry, though. I'll keep my eyes open, and if I see a likely tree, I'll ride out on Monday and get it."

Polly couldn't help smiling back at him. Pa's thoughtful frown may have dulled the radiance of that smile a little, but not much. Jacob Tierney was the sweetest man she'd ever met.

Chapter 3

The next morning at precisely ten fifteen, Polly stood with her mother on the front stoop and waved to Jacob and Billy Clyde as the stage pulled out, heading east.

"Thank you again for looking for a tree," she called, and Jacob touched his whip to his hat brim in reply.

Polly let out a big sigh and leaned back against the doorjamb.

"He's a nice young man," Ma said.

Polly tried to guard her expression, but Ma could always read her. "Sure, he is. He's polite, hardworking, and considerate."

"Not to mention long on looks."

"Ma!" Polly knew her cheeks were red. She ducked inside and began to clear the dishes left by the latest batch of passengers. No matter what time the stage arrived, they always got "dinner." Ma made sure the travelers got their money's worth, too. Today's chicken pie and spice cake had disappeared like magic—the same as every Saturday.

"Well, we'd best change the sheets out back," Ma

said as she came in and shut the door. Every time the driver and shotgun rider left and the incoming pair took their place, Ma changed their beds. When bad weather prevented her from doing laundry, she stripped the beds anyway and kept each bundle of sheets separate, so that when the men returned, they could at least sleep in their own linen, not someone else's. If Billy Clyde were to be believed, this was not the case at every home station. In the summer, when things were busy, he'd sworn one station agent hadn't changed the beds for all of June and July, regardless of who slept in them.

The chores tired Polly out, and she was glad the next day would be their day of rest. The tenders, Harry, and the shotgun messenger who accompanied him—Lyman Towne—did not share the Winfields' faith or Pa's belief that Sunday should be a day of rest and contemplation. They came for their meals on that day and, for the most part, avoided the house the rest of it. Ma said they probably carried on with the poker games in the barn, even on the Lord's Day, but Polly had never ventured to find out.

After breakfast and the kitchen work were done on Sundays, Polly sat with her parents in the parlor. Pa would read scripture for an hour. Then they would pray aloud for all their kinfolk back East, for daily sustenance, for the safety of the drivers and shotgun riders, and for the souls of the tenders. Today Pa's petition for Roberts was especially fervent, and Polly wondered what the man had done now.

After the amen, she opened her eyes.

"Pa, why don't you just fire him?"

"Who?" her father asked, as though he hadn't a clue.

"Roberts. If he's so bad. . ."

"Never you mind, missy."

"Really, Russell," Ma said. "Polly may be right. If he vexes you so. . ."

Pa sighed. "I suppose he's no worse than most—at least most that are available out here. I found an empty whiskey bottle in the hay, and he admitted it was his. Seems he's been having Towne bring him bottles on the Saturday run."

"You'd be justified in letting him go," Ma said.

"But no one will come to replace him this time of year."

Ma shook her head. "No matter. The stages will stop soon. You can get by for a couple of weeks."

"I'll think about it."

After dinner, Polly was allowed to go to her room and read, and she took a nap before joining her mother to prepare supper. On Sunday evening they put out bread, meat, cheese, fruit preserves, and pickles, and the men were invited to help themselves while the family ate in the kitchen.

Harry, Lyman, and Ernest, the other tender, came in to fill their plates, and Polly took them a pitcher of water and the coffeepot.

"Where's Roberts tonight?" she asked.

"Oh, he ain't feeling up to snuff," Ernest said.

When Polly went back to the kitchen, she told her father.

"I'll see about that." He shoved back his chair.

"Oh, Russell, finish your food," Ma said. "If the man is drunk, he'll still be that way when you're done."

"Yes, but the others will go back out there once they've had their cake and coffee. I'd rather speak to him alone."

Pa went out, and Polly looked at her mother. "Do you think it's safe for him to confront Roberts alone?"

"I expect so." Ma frowned, but continued eating as though nothing was wrong, so Polly did the same.

About ten minutes later, to her relief, the front door opened, and Pa's voice carried in from the dining room.

"Boys, just so's you know, I'm discharging Roberts. He'll be going out with you Wednesday, Harry."

"Yes sir," Harry said, as though he had expected this and it bothered him not at all.

"And Towne?"

"Yes, Mr. Winfield?" came the apprehensive response.

"I shall report your actions to the division agent. It will be up to him whether to discipline you or not, but if you ever bring in liquor for any of the stage line's employees again, you'll be out."

"Yes sir."

Pa came into the kitchen. "You heard?" he asked.

Ma nodded. "You can help Ernest with the teams until we get someone else."

"Yes, and Jacob will pitch in when he's here. Probably Harry will, too."

Pa finished his supper, and the family spent a quieter evening than usual, even for Sunday. Polly finished knitting one of the wool socks she was making for her father. The difficulty in making the heel gave her second thoughts about knitting a pair for Jacob. She wanted to do something for him, since he was being so nice about the tree. Would socks be too personal a gift for a young man? She'd better ask Ma before she went ahead with that plan. Anyway, as soon as Pa's socks were finished, she wanted to start making ornaments for her tree.

⁂

The stagecoach arrived on time Sunday at the station near the fort, after a long, cold run from Winfields'. Jacob attended chapel at the fort and spent the rest of the day resting, reading, and talking to the other people at the Newton Station, which was his home on that end of the run. The drop in temperature overnight ruined his plans to search for Polly's Christmas tree on Monday.

"A man shouldn't set out in this cold if he doesn't have to," Mr. Newton, the station agent, said. "In fact, I pity the drivers if they have to bring the stage along today."

"They won't stop it, will they?" The thought that the line would be suspended early for the winter and he might never get back to the Winfields' made Jacob unaccountably sad.

"Not yet," Mr. Newton said. "They'll stop it when the snow gets deep, but not before."

"Too bad we don't have some of Mrs. Winfield's soapstones here," Billy Clyde said.

"How's that?" Jacob asked.

"The passengers complained so much of the cold last year in the fall that she ordered half a dozen soapstones. She'll heat 'em and wrap 'em in burlap and rent 'em to passengers for two bits. It'll be up to you to collect 'em at the end of the stage and get 'em back to her. Norm had that job last year. I think they only lost one, and Mrs. Winfield made a tidy sum. A little extry, she'd say."

Jacob smiled. "Sounds like a good investment. Does she give one to drivers?"

"If the passengers don't take 'em all," Billy Clyde said. "Of course, if you was on her good side—or Miss Polly's—you might get special treatment."

Jacob laughed. He wouldn't butter up Mrs. Winfield or flirt with her daughter to gain special favors, but maybe he could work something out to keep his feet warm. He had a little chat with Mr. Newton later that day.

The mercury stayed close to zero during his whole layover at Newton's home station, but only about three inches of snow fell. By the time the westbound stage pulled in on Tuesday, the road had been packed down enough so that they could travel at their usual pace most of the way, and the horses were eager to go. Jacob was glad to be heading for the Winfields' again. He only wished he wasn't going empty-handed.

Mr. Newton came out as Billy Clyde loaded the last

of the three passengers' luggage. He handed Jacob two bundles.

"What's this?" Billy Clyde asked when he climbed up to the driver's box beside Jacob.

"Hot bricks wrapped in burlap sacks. They won't stay hot as long as Mrs. Winfield's soapstones, but it will help."

The warmth from the bricks did keep the soles of their boots warm for the first five miles or so. When they got to the next swing station, Jacob asked the agent to let him put them on top of his stove during the brief stop. They didn't have time to heat thoroughly, but every bit of warmth helped on the two to three hours between stations.

By the time they approached the third stop, Jacob's fingers were nearly frozen inside his gloves. He could barely hold the reins. He could still feel his toes, though, thanks to the bricks. Even so, the extra warmth in them was long since sapped by the bitter cold.

Jacob awkwardly took the reins in his right hand and put his left hand to his face so he could blow on his fingers through the gloves. He couldn't wear mittens on this job, or he wouldn't be able to handle the reins of the six-horse hitch properly.

Billy Clyde, from beneath layers of the muffler

wound about his neck and face, said, "I sure wish I'd ordered me a soapstone."

"I put in an order for two," Jacob said. "Mr. Newton will send it with his supply order to St. Louis on the next eastbound."

"One for me?" Billy Clyde asked.

"If you want to pay for it. Three dollars, with the shipping."

Billy Clyde blinked at him. "That's a lot."

"If you don't want to buy it, I'll use one for my hands, too."

"I'll think about it," Billy Clyde said.

Jacob would have smiled, but his lips felt frozen. He'd have to grease them with lard at the next station. Billy Clyde wasn't known for saving his pay for anything. He spent it on whatever took his eye at the moment.

"Polly's gonna be disappointed," Billy Clyde said a little later. He had his hands tucked under his arms and had stood his shotgun between his knees, pointing up. If they were held up, Billy Clyde would be sadly unprepared. Of course, most road agents wouldn't be out in this cold to rob stagecoaches anyway.

"I wish I could have gotten her that tree," Jacob said.

"Only one more run to their place before Christmas."

"I know." Jacob concentrated on shifting the reins to his left hand, so he could blow on the right. Two more miles to the next way station. The passengers weren't complaining, but he was certain they would be glad when they got to Winfields' and ate a fine hot meal and had the opportunity to rent a soapstone. A person had to be crazy to travel in this cold.

∞

Polly waited eagerly for the stage on Wednesday. Half a dozen times she went to the window between her tasks of setting up the dining room. Ma caught her at it when she brought in the butter and jelly for the biscuits.

"They'll be here," Ma said, "but they won't come any faster with you gawking out the window."

"It's so cold."

"Not so cold as yesterday, and your father says the road is passable. They'll be here."

The stage pulled in a half hour later than usual, a rare event on the line. The passengers hurried in and huddled around the stove. Billy Clyde and Jacob didn't linger outside but gladly turned the team over to the tenders while the passengers moved to the table to get their meal down before Harry called them to board. Jacob and Billy Clyde stepped closer to the stove and warmed themselves thoroughly.

"The going was a little heavy in spots," Jacob said, flexing his hands above the stovetop, "and the creeks were frozen, but the horses broke through on some of the ice. It wasn't deep, but the wheels tore it all up. That's hard on the team."

"Looked like the off wheeler had a cut on his fetlock," Billy Clyde said mournfully.

Jacob nodded. "Soon's they get the new team hitched and I can feel my fingers, I'm going out and check on them. Some of the horses might need some doctoring."

"The tenders will do it," Billy Clyde said.

Jacob shook his head. "I want to see to them myself."

One of the passengers called for more coffee, and Polly moved to get the coffeepot. "Pa's been keeping the horses inside this week."

"That's good," Jacob said, "but I don't envy Harry and Lyman going out on this next run."

Polly went about her duties. Ma came in while the three passengers ate dessert and offered to rent them a hot soapstone. The men willingly accepted her offer and thanked her fervently.

"Just be sure you give them to the driver when you

get out at his last stop," Ma said. "He brings them back to me. I'm sorry you can't get one at every station."

Ten minutes later, the coach pulled out with all three men aboard, and Harry Smith and Lyman Towne on the box with two of the extra soapstones. Pa came inside with his eyes glinting. Even though fewer passengers rode today, between the dinners and the stones, Ma was turning a profit.

Not until the dishes were done and the dining room swept did Polly broach the subject of the Christmas tree. Pa had invited Jacob and Billy Clyde into the parlor, which was much warmer than their bunk room at the back of the house, and the checker game was in play once more, between Jacob and Billy Clyde. Pa sat on the settee, leafing through a newspaper that Billy Clyde had brought from the other end of the run.

"What's going on in the world, Pa?" Polly asked, taking a seat beside him.

"Well, this is a month old, so it's mostly election news."

"We already knew General Grant was elected," Polly said.

"Yes, but they have a lot of rhetoric about the new governors and Congressmen, too," Pa said, turning the page. "Looks like Spain has tossed out its queen, and she'll be spending Christmas in France—in exile."

"That wasn't very nice of them." Polly looked at Jacob, who was studying the checkerboard. "Speaking of Christmas, I don't suppose you were able to get me a tree, Jacob?"

He looked so remorseful that she wished she hadn't asked.

"No, and I'm sorry."

"Please don't let it distress you," she said quickly. "I understand."

"Thank you."

Her father lowered the newspaper and gazed at Jacob. "Don't look on it as a critical task, Tierney. No one expects you to freeze to death getting a Christmas tree."

"That's right," Polly said. "If it were a simple thing, Pa would have done it."

Her father harrumphed and went back to his reading.

Polly reached for her workbag and took out her knitting. Likely she would have to do without her tree. If they got another snow, Jacob would probably not return.

∞

Jacob enjoyed the next two days, spent quietly with

the family. The tree was not mentioned again, and he tried not to think about it. Mr. Winfield was right—it wouldn't do any good to feel guilty about it. Meanwhile, he spent several pleasant interludes conversing with Polly, usually under the sharp eye of her mother.

He and Billy Clyde ate their dinner early on Saturday and got their gear ready to leave. Jacob went to the barn and inspected the team himself. They all seemed in fine shape and ready for the road. The weather had turned, and the breeze was once more warm and inviting. The snow had melted on the road and shrunk down in other places. So long as the wind stayed light, the next run should not be too unpleasant.

He wandered into the dining room. He had nothing to do until the stage arrived. Then he could grease the wheels. Some drivers let the tenders do that, but Jacob had learned from old Norm that it paid off for the driver to do it himself and know it was done right.

Polly was setting up the long table for the passengers. She always set it for eight after the family and crew had eaten, though often these days fewer travelers came on the coach.

The stage pulled in on time, with Harry sounding a blast of his horn.

Jacob sidled into a corner and watched six

passengers come in. So, quite a few men were taking advantage of the break in the cold and hoping to get across the plains without too much discomfort.

"What kind of place is this, that you don't serve beer?" one man snarled at Polly as he unbuttoned his overcoat.

"It's a decent home where you'll find a welcome and a good hot meal, sir," she replied. "Let me bring you a glass of sweet cider with your dinner."

The man frowned but accepted the offer. Polly looked Jacob's way as she turned away from the disgruntled man, and she smiled at him. Jacob smiled back and clapped his hat on his head. High time he tended to the grease pot.

The Winfield Station was beginning to seem like home—the closest he'd had to a home for the last three years, anyway. Mrs. Winfield mothered him, while her husband treated him like a responsible man who was welcome in the family circle. And Polly made it extra special.

Despite occasional moments when she seemed younger than her eighteen years, Jacob couldn't think of her as a child. She helped her mother willingly, not in sulky obedience, but as a work partner for the business, and she handled unhappy passengers with grace.

Her request for a Christmas tree had amused him at first, but it meant a lot to her, and he knew it wasn't just a childish whim. Having the tree would make her feel more settled in this wilderness.

He still had one more run before Christmas—provided the weather didn't turn nasty again. Mr. Winfield might think it frivolous, but Jacob determined as he mounted the driver's box to get that tree and deliver it on time.

Chapter 4

The following Wednesday, Polly fidgeted more than usual. She and her mother prepared dinner for twelve, though they had no assurance the stage would come. Her father went out to the barn several times during the morning to help Ernest get everything ready. Each time he returned to the kitchen, his predictions were more dire.

"The sky is low and black to the south and west, and the wind is picking up. I'm afraid we'll see snow anytime now."

"But if it's to the west, the stage will be ahead of it," Ma said. "They're coming from the east, so they should get this far all right."

Pa frowned and looked out the window. "They might not have sent the stage out. They don't want the passengers to be stuck here for weeks. If they don't think they can get all the way through, they might not set out."

So this is it, Polly thought. Jacob would not return. She wouldn't get her Christmas tree, and the family would celebrate the holiday without him or Billy Clyde. Funny how her heart ached more to see Jacob than for her precious tree. Two weeks ago, she could think of hardly anything but that tree.

The festive table would feel empty. Roberts was gone. They would invite Ernest, the lone tender remaining, to eat Christmas dinner with them. He wanted to leave for the winter, and he'd planned to go out on this week's eastbound stage. Then it would be just the family here. Pa would have to tend the stock alone. If by some miracle the stagecoaches kept running, he would have to change the teams by himself. Polly supposed she could dress in her cold weather clothing and help him, and the drivers and shotgun riders would pitch in if needed, in an attempt to keep the schedule.

"This is why Butterfield used the southern route," Pa said glumly. "When people send mail out, they expect it to get through."

The stage company had a hard time making a profit on this line. The Winfields did everything they could to ensure good service and keep the line running. After all, this was their livelihood.

About eleven o'clock, the snow began. Small flakes plummeted down, so thick Polly couldn't see to the barn.

"This means business," Pa said.

They went on with the dinner preparations, but as noon approached they feared they would have no guests that day.

Ernest came into the house and stamped his feet on the rag rug by the door. "The team's all set—harnessed and ready to go—but I doubt they'll be coming, Mr. Winfield."

Pa sighed. "I fear you're right, Ernest. Let's sit down and have our dinner."

Ma ladled out generous portions of the stew. Probably they would eat it for the next three days, since she had made much more than the four of them needed.

"I held back on the biscuits," she said. "If the stage comes in, I'll throw more in the oven."

"I sure hope they're not out there in this storm," Ernest said a few minutes later.

They'd all been thinking it, but nobody liked hearing the words.

Polly stood. "I'll start the dishes. Call me if they make it."

"They might surprise us," Ma said. She got up and helped Polly clear and reset the table.

In the kitchen, Polly filled the dishpan and put more water on the stove to heat. Ma went about putting away the food, but Polly noticed that she made a full pot of fresh coffee and set it on the stovetop.

They worked in silence. When Polly had washed all the tableware and begun to scrub the pans, she said, "You don't think they're out there in the snow somewhere, do you?"

"Of course not," Ma said. "If they left the fort last night, they're probably holed up at one of the swing stations. I don't know if Jacob has the experience for it, but Billy Clyde's old enough to know when a storm is coming."

"He said once he can taste snow in the air before it falls," Polly said. She would miss Billy Clyde this winter, too. "I made presents for them."

Ma smiled. "So did I. A vest for each of them. Did you make socks?"

"No. I barely got Pa's done. I made a tobacco pouch for Billy Clyde and a muffler for Jacob. You saw the gray and white yarn."

"Oh, yes, and a muffler's much quicker than a pair of stockings."

"Much simpler, too," Polly said. She'd had trouble turning the heels on Pa's socks, and her mother had helped her redo them.

"Ma, this was going to be the last run."

"I know, dear. Likely the division agent canceled it."

Polly sighed and walked to the stove for a dipperful of hot water. She poured it over the clean biscuit pan to rinse off the soap. "I'll try not to fret about it, but I keep thinking of them all huddled in a stagecoach in some snowdrift, slowly freezing to death."

She tackled the stewpot then dried all the clean dishes. Ma helped her put them away.

"Want me to take the things off the dining table?" Polly asked.

"Let's leave the place settings, just in case. If no one shows up by suppertime, we'll put it all away."

Pa opened the door from the family parlor. "Bertha, I thought I'd saddle my horse and ride down the road a ways."

"In this storm?" Ma's eyebrows shot up almost to her hairline.

"The snow's let up some," Pa said.

"How much is on the ground?" Polly asked.

"Three or four inches so far. They could make it through that, with a stout team. But I doubt they ever left the fort. I just want to make sure."

"Let me come with you, Pa." Polly tossed her apron onto its peg.

He frowned. "I don't know, Polly. It's cold, and you're not dressed for it."

"I'll bundle up. Wait for me, please? I won't be long."

She dashed to her room and opened her top dresser drawer. She had a long, thick pair of woolen stockings that she wore in coldest weather. She pulled them on over her regular stockings and added a pair of sturdy cotton pantalets. They were old-fashioned things, but in extreme times, warmth was more important than fashion.

Knowing her father was waiting, she jerked on a second petticoat—this one flannel—beneath her skirt. A hood, a muffler, boots, her thick woolen coat, and mittens lined in lamb's fleece completed her ensemble.

She ran back to the kitchen. Her mother was putting food into a basket.

"Where's Pa?" Polly asked.

"He went out to saddle the horses. Take these things."

She placed a small box in the basket, tucked a clean towel over the top, and handed it to Polly. "There's a few bandages and things in that little box. And here's your pa's canteen, full of water. Now, Polly, you be careful. And do whatever your father says."

"I will." Polly scurried through the dining room

and outside. The chilly air snatched her breath, and she slowed down. The snow still fell, and the ground, the roofs, even the fence posts, were frosted in several inches of white fluff. The only tracks were those Pa had made. Polly tried to walk in them, but her stride was shorter than his, and the heavy basket threw her off balance. At least the snow was not deeper than her boot tops. Lifting and setting each foot carefully, she made her way to the barn.

Inside, the air was warmer. The fresh team of horses for the coach stamped in their stalls. Pa's horse, Ranger, was already saddled and tied to an iron ring in the wall. In the dimness, Polly made out Pa, saddling the buckskin mare she sometimes rode, and Ernest throwing a blanket across the back of a mule from the extra team they kept on hand, in case anything happened to the horses regularly used on this run.

"Are you going with us?" Polly asked Ernest.

"Thought I would. Getting a little batty just sitting inside all day."

"We're only going a mile or two down the track," Pa said. "I don't want your mother to be left home worrying about us very long."

Polly nodded and carried the basket over to him.

"What's this?"

"Things Ma packed. Food, mostly, and medical supplies."

Pa sighed and pulled the dish towel off the top of the basket. "Have you got saddlebags on your rig?" Pa called to Ernest.

He shook his head.

"Well, take the canteen." Pa nodded at Polly, and she took the water over to Ernest.

When she got back to her father's side, he was tying the basket as securely as he could to the back of Lucy's saddle. He already had a blanket rolled up and tied to the cantle of Ranger's. "Try not to jostle this too much."

He handed her Lucy's reins and led his gelding to the large rolling door. When he pushed it back, a gust of wind blew in, bringing a cloud of swirling snow. Polly adjusted her muffler so that it covered most of her face and led Lucy outside. Ernest brought his mule out and rolled the door shut behind them. Already, the snow seemed deeper than when Polly had come to the barn. A skim of fresh flakes had softened her footprints into dimples in the surface.

"Need a boost?" Pa asked.

Usually Polly didn't, but with all her extra clothing weighing her down, she decided it might help.

"If you don't mind."

She got her foot to the stirrup, and Pa helped her bounce up into the sidesaddle.

"All set?"

She nodded. The harsh wind blew snowflakes into her eyes, and she blinked at them.

"Having second thoughts?"

"No," she said. "I want to go."

Pa hesitated. "All right, but we won't stay out long, like I said. That wind won't be kind to us."

He and Ernest mounted, and the three of them set out, with Ranger and Pa breaking trail. The snow drifted before the angry wind, sometimes making a sheet in front of Polly that nearly prevented her from seeing Ranger's black tail. At other moments, she could see for yards all around. Small eddies of wind picked up snow and whirled it around before dropping it again. She couldn't tell how much new snow was still descending until she looked up and saw myriad flakes falling, always falling.

A huge boulder loomed beside the trail. That landmark told Polly they had come a mile from the house. The small part of her face exposed to the wind began to feel stiff, and the cold seeped through her sturdy boots and layered socks. She clamped her teeth together so they wouldn't chatter, but she wasn't sure how long she could keep this up.

By the time they rounded the bend that was another half mile along, she wondered if they had made a mistake. The snow was coming down harder, and she could barely make out Pa's white-covered form ahead. Lucy plodded along with her head down. Polly didn't want to stop Pa, but she didn't want them to get off the trail and lose the way, or to be overcome by the cold and unable to return home.

Her unease grew, and just as she was about to shout to her father over the wind, Ranger stopped, and Lucy nearly ran into his hindquarters. She stopped, too. Polly clucked to her and pressed her leg against Lucy's side to ease her up next to Ranger.

Pa said nothing, but raised his arm and pointed ahead, down the trail. Polly squinted. A shadowy figure materialized out of nothing, then disappeared again behind a whoosh of snowflakes propelled by the wind.

"Hey!" Pa's shout was blown back at them by a gust, but the cloud of snow passed, and now the form was closer—so close that Polly jumped.

A muffled cry reached them, and they waited. She could see now that a large horse was coming toward them, and hunched over, clinging to its back, was a person. Only when the horse's nose nearly touched

Ranger's could she tell that it was one of the regular coach horses, still wearing his harness. The man perched on his back, clutching one of the straps and a handful of mane, was Jacob.

Chapter 5

"What happened?" Pa yelled.

Jacob leaned toward them. "Wreck!"

"How far?"

"Maybe a mile."

Polly shivered. A mile might as well be a thousand in this storm. At least the stage was closer to the Winfields' than to the next station.

"Anyone hurt?" Pa bellowed, and she realized the wind had momentarily dropped.

Ernest edged his mule up next to Lucy so he could hear what was said.

"Two of them are bad," Jacob said. "I would have set out sooner, but I stayed to build a fire for them."

"Billy Clyde?"

"He fell on his arm, but he's trying to help the others."

Pa nodded. "How many horses do you have?"

"Two more that can travel," Jacob said. "I only set out with four, though I asked for six."

Polly grimaced. That meant one horse was

badly injured or dead.

"I'd have brought people along on them, but I wasn't sure I could make it through," Jacob said. "Figured they'd do better to stick together."

The wind picked up again, howling about them and driving a maelstrom of snow into their faces. Polly ducked her chin and closed her eyes until the worst of it had passed, but its icy fingers pierced even her woolen coat now.

"How many people in all?" Pa shouted.

"Seven passengers and Billy."

"Ernest and I will go back for the oxen and the sled."

That made sense to Polly. More than six inches of snow now covered the ground, and it was drifting much deeper in some spots. But the oxen Pa was fattening to sell in the spring could break through it. They would go slowly, and it might take them a couple of hours to reach the stranded travelers, but Pa would see to it. The injured passengers could ride on the sled that he used in winter to haul supplies and firewood.

Jacob nodded. "I'll stay with the stage."

"Can I go with Jacob?" Polly yelled.

Pa frowned at her then said to Jacob, "Can she get warm if she stays with you?"

"Fuel is hard to come by," Jacob said, "but there are

a few scrub trees. I think we can keep the fire going until you come back if we burn the broken tongue off the coach."

Pa's eyes flickered, and he hesitated. Burning the equipment was a drastic step, but people were badly injured, and the tongue would have to be replaced anyway, by the sound of things.

"All right. Polly, take the food and this blanket." They transferred the items from Ranger's saddle and the canteen from Ernest's.

"We'll try to be there in two hours," Pa said. "It may take longer. Don't give up on us."

"I could send some of the passengers out on the coach horses," Jacob said.

Pa swiveled in the saddle and gazed at their back trail. "They might not be able to see our prints all the way. It's blowing and drifting something fierce."

"I could send Billy Clyde with them. He knows this trail better'n just about anyone."

Pa nodded. "Do it. We won't stick around waiting for them, but we'll look for them on our way back with the ox team."

Polly watched Pa and Ernest ride off, back toward the station. She was shocked by how suddenly they disappeared into blowing snow. The wind howled around her and Jacob.

"We'd better get moving," he said.

"I'll follow you." She had to shout again to make him hear. He pivoted the coach horse. The big animal seemed clumsy compared to Lucy. Riding close behind, Polly had the benefit of shelter. The coach horse's body broke the force of the wind. She huddled low. Lucy didn't need much guidance now. She followed the bigger horse, walking in the trail he had carved in the new snow. They plodded on for what seemed a long time.

Polly grew so cold she thought about unrolling the blanket Pa had given her and wrapping it around her, over her coat. She looked ahead at Jacob's back, wondering if she could make him hear her. Then, to one side and still a ways ahead, she saw a warm orange glow and took heart.

The horses slogged along slowly until they came to the fire. It had burned low, and Polly could see that for lack of fuel it would soon go out. A few yards away, the stagecoach lay on its side. One wheel looked hopelessly smashed, with several of the spokes broken.

"We got off the trail in the storm," Jacob said. "Ran over some rocks. The front axle's bent. It's my fault."

Before Polly could reply, he turned toward Billy Clyde and the seven passengers huddled around the fire and shouted, "This is Polly Winfield, from the next station. I met her and her father and another fellow. Mr. Winfield and Ernest are headed back to the station for an ox team and sled, so we can carry the injured people in."

Several of the passengers got to their feet, staring at Polly, as if she were a ghost appearing out of the snowstorm.

Billy Clyde came over, holding on to his left arm just below the shoulder. "Miss Polly, you oughtn't to be out here! We're like to freeze to death."

"We brought you some sandwiches and water." Polly ignored his dire prediction and swung the canteen toward him. "I have a blanket, too. You can put it over the two hurt folks."

"That sounds mighty good," Billy Clyde said. "I'd help you down, but I think my arm's busted."

"I'm sorry." Polly didn't need any help swinging down off Lucy's back, and in a moment she stood beside him in the snow.

"We need more fuel for the fire," Jacob said. "Mr. Thomas and Mr. Percival, could you help me, please? Mr. Winfield said we can burn the broken wagon tongue. I don't have an axe, but we can burn the two pieces that broke off from the end." He looked at Billy

Clyde. "Let Miss Polly warm herself."

Polly hated displacing anyone at the meager fireside, but she couldn't deny that she needed the heat. Her fingers began to warm soon, but what little warmth radiated from the remains of the fire didn't penetrate her woolen skirts or her boots. The poor fire flickered, and the flames threatened to die.

"It needs more kindling," she said.

"We busted up all the branches we could find," one of the passengers said, and Polly realized the speaker was a woman.

"Ma'am, are you hurt?"

"No, but my husband is. He was thrown from the stage. Thank you for bringing the blanket. I'll put it over him and Mr. O'Neal."

"I've got bandages, too," Polly said. "Perhaps that would help."

"It would indeed."

Polly hurried to her horse and took the basket down. "They're in here, with some food my mother sent." She handed the basket to the woman. "Could you please ask someone to distribute the food? There are a few sandwiches, and some apples and oatmeal cookies."

"That sounds wonderful," the woman said. "I'm Mrs. Ricker."

"I'm sorry you're not enjoying my mother's hospitality this minute, ma'am. But if you'll see to passing out the food, I'll scrounge around and see if I can find anything else burnable. Jacob will need something smaller to feed the fire, if he wants it to catch on to that broken wagon tongue."

The men had struggled with the equipment while she spoke, and now Jacob came to the fire carrying a five-foot piece of the broken timber.

"We need something else," he said, eyeing the smoldering embers.

"I was just going to look for more fuel," Polly said.

"All right. Stay within sight of us. And do you have anything we can use for a sling for Billy Clyde's arm?"

Polly thought for a moment. "There's a towel covering the food in my basket. Ask Mrs. Ricker for it."

Jacob nodded and pointed beyond the overturned stagecoach. "There were a few scrub trees over that way. But I meant what I said about staying close. We don't want to lose you."

She went in the direction he indicated, wading in snow that was nearly as deep as her boots now. She rounded the coach and stared at the luggage spilling from the boot. Tied to the roof of the coach, which was now vertical, was a bushy form that could only be one thing. Jacob had brought her Christmas tree.

❦

Jacob helped Mrs. Ricker tend her husband and the other injured man, Mr. O'Neal. Meanwhile, Polly went off into the darkness. Two of the able-bodied passengers helped her look for wood and they came back with enough small branches among them to perk up the fire until it took hold of the wagon tongue. Everyone couldn't get around the small blaze at once, so they took turns, with the two seriously injured men on one side of the fire, huddled under the blanket, and the others standing around the circle, extending their hands toward the flames.

"It was kind of your mother to send food," said Mr. Percival, a drummer from Kansas City.

"She was happy to do it," Polly said.

Billy Clyde, who was now wearing the towel tied about his neck for a sling, came over to stand beside Jacob. "I could make it to the station on one of those horses."

"Yes, I think you could," Jacob said. "Take Percival and Thomas and head out, while Mr. Winfield's tracks are still visible. I'll wait here with the others." He ticked them off mentally—Mrs. Ricker, the two badly injured men, along with two other fellows who had received no more than a good shaking up and a bruising. They would probably want to know why they couldn't be the ones to ride the horses to the way station, but they hadn't been as ready to help out as Percival and Thomas, so Jacob thought those two had earned the privilege.

"What about Polly?" Billy Clyde asked.

"I'll ask her if she wants to go." Jacob walked over to where Polly stood.

Her smile gleamed in the firelight. "I was thinking that we might do well to build a snow wall around the patients, to shelter them from the wind. It's not too bad right now, but it could pick up again."

"I'm sending Billy Clyde and two others off on the three good coach horses," Jacob said. "Do you want to take your mount and go with them?"

Polly hesitated. "I'd rather stay here, if you think I could be of some help."

"I do. You've already been very helpful, and I'm sure Mrs. Ricker is glad to have some female company. But it may be some time before your father gets back here with those oxen. You could go along with Billy now and be safe at home."

Polly's smile looked a bit sad. "I should feel very guilty if I did that, and I would go wild, wondering if you were all right."

Her words warmed Jacob's heart, though he told himself she meant all of them, not just him.

"All right."

Polly glanced toward where the team stood, and then away. Jacob feared the sight of the one dead horse had upset her.

"We had to put him down. That is, Billy Clyde did. He'd broken a leg, and he was screaming awfully."

She nodded, and he wondered if he had said too much.

"Anyway, I'll be back in a few minutes."

She reached out her mittened hand and touched his sleeve. "Tell Billy and the others to warm themselves thoroughly before they set out. It's a good two miles, and it was quite a journey out here."

Jacob helped the three men get the horses ready. Mr. Percival and Mr. Thomas assured him they could ride the two miles without saddles.

"Can't get much colder than we are out here," Thomas said. "I'm game."

Jacob gave Billy Clyde a boost up onto the large wheeler's back. Billy Clyde moaned before he straightened and took the single rein in his good hand.

"You sure you'll be all right?" Jacob asked.

"I'll make it." Billy Clyde clucked to the horse and moved out ahead of the other two.

When Jacob got back to the fire, Mrs. Ricker and the two uninjured men were huddled around it. The others had brought over two large satchels from the luggage boot and were now seated on them.

"Shove that timber in a little farther," Jacob said to one of the men.

Polly was at the fringe of the circle of light, patting snow into a low barrier behind where the sick men lay.

"Is it sticky enough?" Jacob asked.

"I think so. We used to make snow forts when I was a child."

"I'll help you." The wind gusted, throwing a bushel of loose flakes into the air.

Polly shook them off her head.

"It seems awfully flaky and dry for this." Jacob scooped up handfuls and tried to pack a snowball, but it wouldn't hold together. "If we had a shovel. . ."

"We just have to keep at it," Polly insisted.

"Maybe what you're using is closer to the fire." Jacob settled in to work beside her, determined not to quit, no matter what. He hoped the next gale wouldn't blow away their wall. At least this exercise kept Polly moving. The others seemed content to stay seated on their luggage near the fire.

"It could be hours before your father comes back," Jacob said. "I'm thinking of busting up the coach wheels to burn."

"I think we've exhausted the supply of bushes nearby," Polly said.

"Yes. I'm not sure I can break up anything else without tools, though. And I hate to start busting up the coach." Jacob looked toward the damaged stage-coach. The division agent would be upset enough when he heard about the accident, let alone if they burned the whole coach, but the broken wheel at least could be sacrificed.

"There's my Christmas tree," Polly said.

So, she had seen it. He was surprised the passengers hadn't already tried to burn it. "I really don't want to use that," he said. "It's small, and it would burn up fast. I don't think it would do much good, really."

Polly smiled at him. "All right, but if we get desper-ate, it goes on the fire. Agreed?"

"Agreed."

Mrs. Ricker walked over to where they worked.

"I hate to trouble you, Mr. Tierney, but if you could find my husband's valise, he had another jacket in it, and I thought perhaps I could get it on him.

He's shivering violently."

"Of course."

Jacob left Polly to work on the snow wall and went to help Mrs. Ricker. One of the other men came to the overturned coach and helped him retrieve Mr. Ricker's valise. Jacob wrenched three loose spokes from the broken wheel and added them to the fire.

Polly's barrier was now nearly two feet high and about eight feet long. Mr. Ricker and the other injured man were sheltered behind it, and Jacob could feel the difference it made.

Polly smiled up at him. "This work is keeping me warm."

"Good, because I don't think we'll find anything else to burn."

Jacob set to work with her, and they completed a semicircular snow wall that he estimated to be thirty feet long. Toward the last of it, one of the disgruntled men came to help them.

"Might as well move about," he muttered, and began to pack more snow along the top of the barrier.

The fire burned down, but the snow had stopped falling, and the wall helped cut the wind. "Come on over here," Jacob called to the other man, who sat stubbornly near the cooling ashes. Jacob, Polly, the two male passengers, and Mrs. Ricker sat shoulder to shoulder, near the makeshift pallet for the two wounded.

"I suppose we could play Twenty Questions," Polly said.

One of the men laughed at her suggestion, but soon they all joined in, and the grumblers quit complaining.

Jacob judged that two hours had passed since Mr. Winfield left them. Finally, he spotted a speck of light in the distance. He rose stiffly and plodded onto the trail. The tracks of those who had gone on were no longer visible, concealed by drifting snow, but he could still see the contour of the road. Far in the distance was the light he had glimpsed. He was now sure it was a lantern, shining for the oxen that trudged along pulling the sled.

He turned back toward the group. "It's Mr. Winfield. He's coming!"

Polly rose and staggered toward him. Jacob seized her hand and pulled her along through the snow.

"Is it over your boot tops?" he asked.

"I don't know. I can't feel my feet." But she managed to advance toward the ox team.

Mr. Winfield shouted, and when they at last met, Jacob saw that Ernest had returned with him.

"We've got four hot soapstones," Polly's father said.

"Is everyone all right?"

"Nearly frozen," Jacob told him. "We ran out of wood. Bring the sled closer, and I'll help you load the two injured men. Can Mrs. Ricker ride as well?"

"Yes, and there's room for Polly," Mr. Winfield said.

"Pa, if you just let me warm my feet on one of those stones first, I'll ride Lucy back," Polly said.

"If you're sure." Her father eyed her doubtfully. "We met Billy Clyde and the others a mile out from the house. I'm sure they made it in, but those horses were about done."

"You brought the mules," Jacob said, peering through the dimness toward the shadowy forms behind the ox sled. Ernest rode one of the mule team and appeared to have the rest strung together on a lead line.

"They don't like it, but they've come along in the track of the sled. We've got only four, so you decide who rides what."

Jacob helped situate the injured men on the sled while Polly warmed her feet and her father got the other passengers onto mules. Mr. Winfield gave soapstones to Mrs. Ricker to use for the patients, and she settled down to ride beside her husband. Jacob and Ernest took the other two mules, and Polly's father boosted her into Lucy's saddle. The poor little buckskin would be glad to get back to the shelter of the barn, Jacob was sure.

He took a last look back at the stagecoach and remembered one more thing.

"I'll be right back," he told Polly.

He urged his mule over to the side of the coach. It was mostly covered in snow now. By leaning over and scooping off six or eight inches of fluff with his arm, he was able to uncover his prize—the scraggly little tree he'd tied to the top of the vehicle.

His fingers were too stiff to untie the knots, but he took out his knife and sliced through the rope. A moment later, he had the tree dragging behind him. The mule didn't like it, but was too tired to put up much of a fuss.

Polly's eyes were huge above the fold of scarf covering her mouth. "You're going to bring it!"

"Why not?" Jacob said. "After all the trouble I went to to get it, I don't want to leave it behind."

She laughed. "Thank you! Come on, even the oxen are ahead of us."

They started out for the trek through the snow.

Chapter 6

Ma had lanterns burning on the front porch, and lamps cast their cheery light out the dining room windows. Polly's heart cheered when she saw the welcoming glow. Billy Clyde, Mr. Thomas, and Mr. Percival waded out into the yard to meet them.

"Go right in and get warm, folks," Billy Clyde shouted. "Mrs. Winfield's got a roaring fire going, and hot vittles for ya."

Mr. Percival stepped forward to take Lucy's bridle. "Are you all right, Miss Winfield?"

"Yes, thank you."

"Your mother was quite worried about you," he told her.

"I was in good hands, but I'll go right in and show her that I'm safe."

Mr. Thomas and Pa carried Mr. Ricker inside on a woolen blanket. Polly hurried past Jacob, who was untying the rope on his saddle horn so Billy Clyde could take the mule to the barn and unsaddle it.

"Ma," Polly shouted as she entered the house.

Her mother came out of the kitchen, her cheeks rosy and her hands covered with flour.

"Polly! You must be near frozen, child."

"Not so bad." As she unwound her scarf, Polly hurried through to the kitchen stove. The guests could have the fireplace in the dining room, and no doubt her parents would let them into the parlor, too, by the small coal stove. "What can I do to help? We've all these extra people for at least the night, probably longer."

"Yes, I've thought of that. Billy Clyde helped me work out the arrangements." Her mother wiped her hands. "First we'll feed them and get them warm. I shall help with the injured gentlemen if needed. You'll have to sleep in my room with me tonight, dear. We'll give the Rickers your room, and your father can bunk with Jacob and Billy Clyde."

"That makes sense." Polly doffed her mittens and stretched out her aching fingers toward the kitchen range. "What of the others?"

"The men who aren't hurt can sleep in the tenders' room with Ernest. It will be snug, but at least it's warm out there, and we'll have more privacy. The injured ones will have to be in here, where we can care for them."

Polly unbuttoned her coat. "Well, I'm ready to work.

Just tell me what to do."

"Take the biscuits out of the oven and put the sheet cake in. The stew has been simmering all evening. If you can serve it up and give them all hot coffee, I'll distribute bedding. I expect your father will be tied up in the barn for a while, caring for the livestock, but we can make Mrs. Ricker comfortable and provide whatever she thinks will help her husband."

Polly put on her apron and went to work, humming a hymn as she flitted about the kitchen. When she entered the dining room with four steaming soup plates on a tray, the four male passengers who were able were seated at the table, along with Billy Clyde.

"Hungry, gents?" Polly asked with a smile.

"Famished," said Mr. Percival. "Young lady, that smells delicious."

"My mother made it, so of course it is." She set a dish before him and made her rounds of the table, setting a serving before each passenger. "Billy Clyde, I'll bring yours in a trice, along with coffee and biscuits."

"Take your time, missy. It's not like I'll eat more than the tablecloth if you don't hurry."

Polly laughed and scuttled into the kitchen to reload her tray.

By the time the men had eaten their stew and were

starting on the cake, Polly's mother came in from the family quarters carrying an armful of quilts and linen.

"Gentlemen, I apologize for the lack of order here. We don't often have overnight guests."

"You owe us no penance, madam," Mr. Percival said. "We've eaten like kings, and I'm told we'll have a warm place to cast our bedrolls on the floor."

"Yes, there's a stove in the tenders' room," Ma said. "I've brought out every extra blanket and sheet we own, and I'll let you divvy them up as you see fit. We've settled Mr. O'Neal on the parlor sofa so we can keep an eye on him."

"How are he and Mr. Ricker doing?" Billy Clyde asked.

"I think they'll be much better for some warm broth and a good night's sleep," Ma said. "Mr. O'Neal seems to have a broken arm and quite a bump on his head. It's Mr. Ricker I'm more worried about. He appears to have taken a blow to the head when the coach overset, and he's terribly bruised. Broken ribs, I shouldn't wonder."

"Too bad we didn't have a doctor among us," said Mr. Thomas, holding his cup out to Polly for more coffee.

Pa, Jacob, and Ernest came through the front door

after stamping the snow off their feet on the porch.

"Time for the second sitting, gentlemen," Polly told those at the table. "Perhaps Billy Clyde will show you your accommodations."

The four passengers went out carrying the bedding, and some of them their coffee mugs. It seemed very quiet when only Pa, Jacob, and Ernest remained.

"I'll take these dirty dishes off and bring you some stew," Polly said.

"I ate my supper," Pa said, "but I could do with some of that cake, and I expect Jacob wants his stew."

"Whenever it's convenient," Jacob said.

Ernest laughed. "Listen to him. You're too polite, boy!"

Jacob looked a little flustered, but he reached for one of the dirty plates. "Let me help you, Miss Polly."

"Sure," Ernest said. "That way, we'll get our eats quicker."

Polly piled her tray with crockery and flatware, and Jacob came around the table.

"I'll take that out for you. It looks heavy."

Ernest laughed again, and Polly felt her cheeks go scarlet.

"Don't mind him," Jacob said when they reached the sanctuary of the kitchen.

"He's got no manners," Polly said. "I've never once heard him offer to help Ma or me."

"Perhaps he didn't grow up in a home with a nice mother who taught him to be polite and lend a hand," Jacob said.

Polly smiled as she lifted dishes into the dishpan. "I never thought of it that way."

Jacob's return smile made her stomach queasy.

"By the way, I left your tree out on the porch. Didn't want to bring it in with snow all over it. I'll see about it tomorrow, though. Where do you want it?"

"In the parlor, if Mr. O'Neal's not too sick to have us working around him." Polly set the last of the dishes off the tray and took it from him. "Thank you, Jacob. I really appreciate that you took extra trouble to get that tree for me, and that you thought to bring it here from the stage."

"I was glad to do it."

Their gazes held for a moment, and Polly thought she could stare into his twinkling brown eyes forever. Jacob looked away first, a half smile on his lips. "Shall I get my own stew?"

"Oh, I'm sorry. I need to wash a bowl for you. We ran out of dishes tonight."

She washed and dried one of the soup plates and

ladled it full of stew. "I'll bring in the biscuits, but the fresh coffee won't be ready for a few minutes. Would you like water now?"

"That'd be fine." Jacob carried his dish into the dining room. While Polly put the last half-dozen biscuits on the serving plate, her mother came in with another tray of dishes.

"I'm pleased. Mrs. Ricker got her husband to take some broth, and she ate a good supper herself. She's a very sweet woman."

"I hope Mr. Ricker is going to be all right." Polly hesitated then said, "Ma, how does a girl find a husband out here?"

Her mother set her tray on the worktable. "You like Jacob, don't you?"

"Well, yes. Don't you?"

"He's a very nice young man. Oh, Polly, back in Massachusetts, you'd meet suitable young men at church, or in town, or at neighbors' houses. Here we have only those who pass by on the road. So far, I think Jacob is the best of the lot."

"So do I," Polly said, smiling.

"But you must be careful. And your father and I must get to know him better and make sure of his intentions. Just because he is the first decent, eligible man to come along, does not mean he's the one for you."

Polly nodded slowly, but she could barely hold back her smile. "I understand, Ma."

∞

Christmas day dawned cold but sunny, with the Winfields and Jacob eating a hearty breakfast of eggs, sausage, and pancakes. The division agent had sent a crew two days previous with two sleighs, each pulled by six draft horses. They had taken away the stranded passengers. Ernest had gone with them, to spend the winter with his parents near St. Joseph, and Billy Clyde had joined the others in hopes of seeing the fort's doctor about his arm.

Jacob felt a bit awkward as the only guest for the holiday, but the Winfields assured him that he was welcome to stay.

"We've got the stagecoach fixed right as rain," Mr. Winfield said as he helped himself to seconds on sausage and pancakes. "As soon as the roads are good for wheeling again, Jacob will be able to resume his work."

"That's if the line decides to keep me on," Jacob said.

Mr. Winfield reached for the molasses pitcher. "They should. You've proved you can repair your chariot as well as drive it."

Jacob laughed. "I suppose a driver who is handy with tools is an asset to the company."

"Indeed. And I'll put in a good word for you."

When the meal was finished and the dishes done, they gathered in the parlor. Jacob didn't dare sit down beside Polly on the sofa, but took a chair opposite, where he had a good view of her yule tree. She had cajoled him, Billy Clyde, and Ernest into helping her decorate it. Though it came a foot short of the ceiling, and its limbs drooped a little, it now stood resplendent in the corner, reaching its branches into the room, as though offering the popcorn strings and paper stars and angels that festooned it. Mrs. Winfield had brought out six glass ornaments from some recess in the house, and they seemed all the finer because they were few.

Mr. Winfield opened the large family Bible on his lap as his wife settled down beside Polly, her knitting bag in her hands.

"I like to read the second chapter of Luke on Christmas morning," he said.

Jacob nodded. He looked forward to hearing the familiar words once more.

Mr. Winfield held the book up closer to his face and opened his mouth to read.

A loud knock sounded at the front door, followed by Billy Clyde's muffled shout of, "Hello! Anyone home this morning?"

Polly jumped up and hurried out of the room, returning seconds later with Billy Clyde.

"Merry Christmas, folks," the shotgun rider said. "Sorry to interrupt."

"Nonsense," Mrs. Winfield said. "Grab a seat. You're just in time for the scripture reading."

Billy Clyde crossed to sit beside her, on the other end of the couch from Polly, his hat crumpled in his hands.

"Any news, before we begin?" Mr. Winfield asked.

"A few bits. I'm to wear this sling for a month, and Mr. Ricker is on the mend."

"Oh, I'm so glad," Mrs. Winfield said. "What about Mr. O'Neal?"

"He'll recover. He's gone on already, back to Independence. And Jacob—" Billy Clyde fixed his gaze on his friend. "The division agent said to tell you that Mr. O'Neal was a heavy investor in the line."

"You don't say," Mr. Winfield put in.

"I certainly didn't know it," Jacob said.

"He commended you for getting everyone to safety last week," Billie Clyde said, triumph in his eyes.

"You can keep your job, sonny. Don't expect to drive the stagecoach out of here soon, but he wants to send sleigh runs through and see how that works. You're to be ready on Saturday, weather permitting."

"Do you think you'll have many passengers?" Mrs. Winfield asked.

"Probably not, but we've contracted a mail run through to Boise for the next six months."

Polly had kept silent during this exchange, but now she beamed at Jacob. "There! Your job is secure, at least for a while, Jacob."

Mr. Winfield read the chapter, and then he brought out the parcels from beneath Polly's bedraggled little tree. He put the small box Jacob had brought for Polly in her hands, and Jacob held his breath while she opened it.

"Oh! It's lovely." She passed the box to her mother.

"Yes, indeed. Very nice." Mrs. Winfield touched a finger to the silver necklace.

The filigree cross had seemed right to Jacob when he saw it at the trader's on his last run to the fort. Polly looked at him and smiled.

"Thank you. It's beautiful."

Jacob exhaled carefully. Her mother hadn't protested or said the gift was too personal for her daughter to accept. Did that mean Polly's parents would receive him as a suitor for her? He hoped so, because the more time he spent with them, the more he wanted to become part of the family.

Mr. Winfield placed a parcel in his hands, and Jacob turned his attention to it. A striped muffler, knit by Polly herself. The others opened their packages, exclaiming over the thoughtful items each had made or purchased. Jacob had a new vest from the Winfields and a bag of penny sweets from Billy Clyde. But perhaps the nicest gift he received was seeing the pure joy on Polly's face as she sat in the shadow of the Christmas tree.

❧

After supper, Polly couldn't sit still. Jacob and her father had gone to the barn to tend the livestock, and Jacob had told Billy Clyde to stay in the house and rest his poor arm. His look had been so meaningful, and Billy Clyde's answering smile so mischievous, that Polly knew something was up. She wasn't sure she could last until Pa and Jacob returned, and Billy Clyde's teasing didn't help.

"So, you've got some fine jewelry now, missy," he said when her mother had gone to the kitchen for a moment.

"What do you know about it?" Polly said, feigning disinterest.

"Oh, I know heaps," Billy Clyde said.

Stomping footsteps came from outside, and soon Jacob appeared in the doorway. "Any coffee, Polly?"

"Certainly. I'll get it." She jumped up, but Jacob held up a hand to stop her.

"No, I thought maybe Billy Clyde could get it. Your pa said there was more of that pie, too." He looked keenly at Billy Clyde.

"Oh, I'm wanted in the kitchen, am I?" Billie Clyde lumbered up awkwardly from his chair, trying to keep from bumping his injured arm. "Half an hour ago, I was no help, and now you want me to do everything."

"Hush," Jacob said. "Just go make yourself useful."

"I can take a hint." Billy Clyde shuffled toward the kitchen.

Polly hardly dared look at Jacob. Her cheeks were flaming hot, and if asked, she would have to agree that it was very odd for Jacob to clear the room.

"Is everything all right in the stable?" she asked.

"Oh, yes." Jacob stepped toward her. "Polly, I spoke to your father."

"Did you?" She could barely breathe. She gazed up

from beneath her eyelashes. "And?"

"He—he said I could court you. If you wished it. Polly, please say you wish it. I think you're the nicest girl I've ever met, and the way you helped Mrs. Ricker and nearly froze your toes off to build that snow wall . . .well, I think you're wonderful."

Polly laughed, a little giddy from the suddenness of it. "You're no slouch, Jacob Tierney. And I've thought a lot about our talk a couple of weeks ago."

"Have you?"

"Yes."

He stepped closer. "Do you mean when you were telling me all the things you missed about the East?"

She nodded. "I'm ready for Wyoming now. To make this my home. Well, it *is* my home," she hurried on, "but I don't think I'd fully accepted that until after we talked, and until you brought me that silly, beautiful little tree." She looked over her shoulder, smiling, at the Christmas tree. When she turned back toward him, Jacob stepped closer and put his arms around her.

"I'm glad I got snowed in here, and not at the fort."

In the shadow of the Christmas tree, he leaned toward her and kissed her. In the most glorious moment of her life, Polly kissed him back.

"Do you think you might share that Wyoming future with me?" he asked softly.

"Oh, yes," Polly said. "I believe we can make something of it together."

About the Author

Susan Page Davis is the author of more than forty novels, in the romance, mystery, suspense, and historical romance genres. A Maine native, she now lives in western Kentucky with her husband, Jim, a retired news editor. They are the parents of six, and the grandparents of nine fantastic kids. She is a past winner of the Carol Award, the Will Rogers Medallion for Western Fiction, and the Inspirational Readers' Choice Award. Susan was named Favorite Author of the Year in the 18th Annual Heartsong Awards. Visit her website at: www.susanpagedavis.com.

The Evergreen Bride

By Pam Hillman

Chapter 1

The piney woods along Sipsey Creek,
Mississippi, December 1887

Samuel Frazier's heart skittered into double time when Annabelle Denson rushed into the sawmill. She grabbed his arm, her touch sending a jolt of awareness coursing through him.

"Papa said I could go!" Annabelle's evergreen eyes danced beneath the woolen scarf draped over her hair.

Had Pastor Denson given in, then? Samuel looked away, dread filling his chest. "Where?"

Annabelle swatted his arm and moved away to sit on the low stool he'd made just for her. Every day, after she rang the school bell and the Sipsey Creek schoolchildren swarmed out of the schoolhouse and raced toward home, Samuel dusted the sawdust from the stool, hoping she'd stop by on her way home. Most days she did.

"To Illinois, of course. As if you didn't know."

Of course.

It was all she'd talked about for weeks, for months, actually. A trip to Chicago, Illinois, to visit her cousin Lucy. So she could have a white Christmas. He turned away from the excitement on her face, back to the board he'd been working to smooth. He made another swipe at the piece, the scrape of the plane filling the void left by his silence. It wasn't his place to derail Annabelle's dream of a little snow-filled adventure. But maybe when she returned, when he and Jack got the old sawmill fully operational again, he'd get up the nerve. . .

Annabelle tossed the woolen scarf back, and the feeble sunlight streaming through the open shop door landed on hair the same dark mahogany as the hope chest he'd made for her last Christmas. She pulled an envelope from her pocket and waved it in his face. "Aunt Eugenia is going to visit and Papa said I could go, too. He says the train isn't a safe place for a lady traveling alone."

"You don't agree?"

"In this day and age?" Her nose scrunched up, reminding him of Lilly, her two-year-old sister, refusing to eat boiled okra. But, although Annabelle might be cute as a button, she definitely wasn't a child. Not by a long shot. She'd turn twenty next summer. "Goodness,

Samuel, it's almost the turn of the century, and women travel alone all the time these days."

"Some women, maybe, but not the sister and daughter of a respected minister from the Mississippi pine belt." He couldn't resist teasing her. "Maybe Reverend Denson should reconsider."

"Oh no, he's already agreed, so it's settled. He can't change his mind now." Annabelle clasped the letter to her chest with both hands. "My very own white Christmas. It'll be glorious."

The snow couldn't be half as glorious as the glow on her face as she talked about it. Reluctantly, Samuel lowered his gaze and brushed the film of sawdust off the board. Smooth as silk and perfect for a slat in the rocking chair Reverend Denson had ordered for his wife. "But you'll miss Christmas here with—"

With us. With me.

He bit back the words he wanted to say, and finished instead, "—with your family."

"They'll hardly know I'm gone come Christmas morning. And besides, Jack will probably spend the entire day with Maggie's family anyway." She swiveled on the stool. "By the way, where is my brother? I can't wait to tell him my news."

"Gone to take a load of logs to Abe's." He and Jack

snaked logs out of the woods around Sipsey Creek and hauled them to Abe Jensen's sawmill twice a week. Two days lost in travel that could be spent harvesting trees if they had their own circular saw.

"Why does Jack always go?"

"You know Jack." He shrugged. "He likes to be out and about, meeting people. And besides, I've got to finish this rocking chair."

Annabelle stood and ran her hand along one of the rungs of the half-finished chair. "Mama's going to love this."

The scent of rose petals, or lavender, or whatever women tucked between the folds of their clothes in a chest of drawers still clung to her dress even after a day of teaching. Flustered by her nearness, he concentrated on the chair and muttered, "Hope so."

"Of course she will." She dusted off her hands. "Speaking of Mama, I need to get on home and help her with supper. Don't forget to tell Jack my news."

"I'll tell him."

She headed toward the door, but whirled around, cocked her head to one side and studied him, tiny frown lines on her forehead. "You're excited for me, aren't you, Samuel?"

"Of course I am, Annie-girl. It's what you've always

dreamed of." He tossed a handful of sawdust toward her. She dodged away, laughing as she brushed the flecks from the hem of her brown skirt. "Just don't run off up north and forget all about us poor ol' folks here at home."

"I'd never forget y'all." She flashed him a bright smile as she headed out the wide barn-like door he'd propped open to let in a bit of sunlight. "See you Sunday."

Samuel watched her go, her dark skirts swaying with each step. The loblolly pines, with their bright wintergreen needles that towered along each side of the road, marked her path, and he couldn't help but remember how her green eyes lit up with excitement when she told him about her trip.

As she rounded the bend out of sight, the smile slipped from his face and he turned back, his gaze surveying the dilapidated building he and Jack owned. Summer before last, they'd bought it on credit when old man Porter had called it quits. They'd poured every dollar they could into the business, working their fingers to the bone to get it up and running again.

They could fill small orders for lumber by cutting boards with a crosscut saw in a saw pit, but Samuel dreamed of a steam engine and circular saw like Abe's.

They'd never make a decent living with just a crosscut and the sweat of their brow. Porter hadn't been able to make a go of it either. He'd said he couldn't compete with the newfangled saws. But Jack and Samuel were young and eager.

And broke.

But they had dreams of expanding, one step at a time. In the meantime, he'd keep making furniture and hope chests, snaking logs out of the swamp, and hauling them to Abe. But someday, he and Jack would have their own steam-powered saw.

And then he'd court Annabelle.

Chapter 2

As soon as supper was over, dishes washed, and the kitchen spotless, Annabelle excused herself to write a letter to Lucy. An excited buzz built inside as she penned questions, asking her cousin what to pack, how many changes of clothes she would need, how many outings Lucy had planned.

She frowned, thinking about how fashion might be different in Illinois than it was in Mississippi. Was there time for Lucy to send her a couple of catalogs of the latest styles? She tapped her pencil against the letter, thinking. Between teaching and helping her mother around the house, she didn't have time to make a new dress. She'd just have to make do. Scrapping the idea of a new outfit, she continued her letter, urging Lucy to ask her father about accompanying Annabelle back home to Mississippi.

Lucy, you really should come for a visit. It's been seven years since you moved away. You tell me that none of the young men there catch your fancy. Well, there are plenty here that I think you'd do well to set your cap for.

Do you remember Amos Rosenthal? He's taking over his father's dry goods store and would be a good catch. And Willie Godfries started working for the railroad just last week. No, never mind about Willie. From what I've heard, he's a bit wild, although I shouldn't say things like that without proof. But as they say, where's there's smoke, there's fire.

Annabelle studied her letter, trying to think of someone else that would entice Lucy to come back to Mississippi. She grinned. If her cousin came for a visit and just happened to fall in love with someone local, then they'd get to see each other all the time.

Her gaze landed on the hope chest in the corner of her room.

Samuel.

Oh my goodness! Why hadn't she thought of it before? Samuel would be perfect for Lucy. She chewed her pencil, trying to think of a way to describe her brother's partner and best friend. Her words filled the page.

I have the most perfect beau in mind for you. Do you remember Jack's partner, Samuel Frazier? He and Jack have started their own business, and he makes the most exquisite furniture. He made my hope chest last Christmas. I'm sure I told you about it. It's so beautiful, and sturdy, too.

But I'm sure you're not interested in the quality of his furniture, are you?

Samuel is tall, but not too tall, mind you. And he's very handsome, at least all the girls say so. Mama would skin me alive if she saw this letter, but he really is just perfect. He does like to tease me, though, and that's a bit bothersome, but it's all in good fun. I don't think he realizes it, but sometimes I can tell when he's teasing because he'll act like he's ignoring me by keeping his hands busy, but then he'll give me this funny little crooked smile.

Annabelle stopped writing and let her thoughts wander back to the afternoon at the sawmill, trying to visualize how Samuel had looked when she'd barged inside. He'd been engrossed in his work, his large hands smoothing a slat for her mother's rocking chair, his hair mussed from a hard day's work, a late afternoon shadow covering his lean cheeks.

She bit her lip.

How could she explain to Lucy how Samuel's dark hair curled over his ears just so, even though he'd been promising to get a haircut for weeks? Or how his brown eyes twinkled when he teased her about her trip to Illinois? Or even how respectful he was when her mother invited him over for Sunday dinner? He always thanked Mama for the meal and never asked for seconds for dessert.

She smiled. But that didn't stop Jack from reaching across the table and cutting two extra large pieces of pie and plopping one on Samuel's plate. Samuel never said a word, just threw her a wink, and gave her his crooked little grin.

Her heart tripped a little at the thought of that grin. Without even trying, he'd probably gotten his way with that dimpled smile from the time he was knee-high to a cricket.

But how to explain all that in a letter to Lucy, in such a way that would make her cousin want to come to Mississippi to visit? She shook her head. She'd just have to tell Lucy more about Samuel when she got there. It shouldn't be too hard to convince her. Pleased with her plan, Annabelle finished her letter and addressed it.

She stored her writing supplies in her hope chest, smiling as she ran her hand over the smooth lid, stained dark and polished to a high sheen. Samuel did make beautiful furniture, and he really did have a nice smile.

He'd be the perfect beau.

Chapter 3

"Timber!"

Samuel scrambled out of the way, Jack right on his heels. They didn't stop until they'd put a safe distance between themselves and the severed pine. Samuel held his breath. Would it fall true?

For a split second, time stood still; then a faint groan wafted across the clearing. The sound sent a shaft of excitement through Samuel's veins, along with a healthy dose of fear in case the tree went wild.

The faint cracking and groaning grew louder until a great rent split the air and the trunk tilted, slowly at first, then gaining speed as it fell toward the forest floor littered with pine needles.

Limbs the size of a man's thigh split and rent the air with cracking, popping noises. Mere seconds later, the long, tall, loblolly pine slapped against the forest floor with a heavy thud that shook the ground where they stood.

Samuel let out his breath and slapped Jack on the back. His partner grinned, wiped the sweat glistening on his brow, and settled his hat more firmly on his head. "Mighty glad that's done."

"Laying 'er down is just the beginning."

"The rest can wait. I'm starving." Jack walked away, and Samuel followed, stomach growling. Come to think of it, lunch did sound like a good idea.

They found the rucksacks they'd hung on a low-lying limb to keep safe from prowling critters and settled in for a well-deserved break. They tucked into thick slabs of ham and leftover biscuits Jack's mother had sent with him that morning.

Samuel swallowed the last of a biscuit and rested his head against the rough pine at his back. If they didn't have to delimb the tree and snake it out to the road, he'd take a short nap right then and there.

"You should see Abe's new circular saw." Jack spread his arms wide. "Forty-eight-inch blade. I've never seen the like."

Samuel snapped to attention. "Did you ask him about his old saw?"

"Yep." Jack picked up a pine needle and threaded it through his fingers. "He'll let us have it for half the profits on the lumber we cut. But we have to dismantle it and haul it ourselves."

"What about the saw blade?"

"Still has all its teeth. All it needs is a good sharpening. You think it's worth it?"

"Maybe." Samuel pondered Jack's question. "Having a circular saw, even one that small, would be better than using the crosscut in the saw pit."

"But on halves? That don't seem rightly fair for Abe to get half of what we make sawing logs."

"It's his saw, and we can't afford to buy it outright." Samuel shrugged. "And besides, he'd keep a tally and eventually we'd own it, fair and square."

"We'd still need bigger machinery eventually, if we're gonna make a go of it."

"Gotta start somewhere."

"I know, but time's a wastin'."

Samuel squinted at his friend. "Maggie?"

"Yeah." Jack tossed the pine needle away, and it bounced off the nearest tree.

"Have you popped the question?"

"Not yet." Jack grimaced as he swiped crumbs from his trousers.

"You know she'll say yes." Why wouldn't she? Jack and Maggie had been courting nigh on to two years now. Everybody expected them to get married. It wasn't a matter of if, but when.

Jack cleared his throat. "I've been meaning to talk

to you about that."

Samuel arched a brow. Jack's gaze met his, then skittered away to focus on the evergreens swaying in the breeze high above their heads. He acted plumb nervous, and nothing fazed happy-go-lucky Jack.

"I can't ask Maggie to marry me without a place to live. And we barely squeaked by last year, what with buying that freight wagon and another pair of mules."

"Is that all that's stopping you?"

"I'd ask her tomorrow if I knew I could provide for her." Jack's eyes took on a look of desperation. "Her pa's been making noises about moving on, out west somewhere."

No surprise there. It was a known fact that Maggie's pa had wandering feet and uprooted his family every couple of years. Jack's reasons for not asking Maggie to marry him were the same ones that kept Samuel from courting Jack's sister, except Samuel had plenty of time to get up the nerve to court Annabelle.

Jack didn't have the luxury of waiting.

"Then let's accept Abe's offer. As soon as we get the saw up and running, we can start cutting lumber to sell, and also stockpile some to build a house for Maggie."

Jack stood, slapped his hat against his pants, and grumbled, "And when are we going to have time to do all this cuttin' and sawin'? We're already working from sunup to sundown."

"You're just gonna have to do less courtin' and more working. Come on, let's get started. If we get this pine snaked out, we'll earmark some more trees before nightfall."

Chapter 4

"Do you think it might snow?" Annabelle asked Maggie as the congregation filed out of church after Sunday morning worship.

"I doubt it." Maggie pulled on a frayed woolen coat and buttoned it up. "It'll just be cold and wet and muddy, but it probably won't snow."

"Jack thinks it will. Here I am headed to Illinois in a couple of weeks and everyone's talking about it snowing here in Sipsey." Annabelle laughed as she settled her scarf over her head. "God sure does have a sense of humor."

"We lived up in the mountains of Tennessee once, and it snowed so much Pa couldn't even get to the barn. I thought I would freeze to death." Maggie's features softened as her attention veered toward Jack standing with the men at the potbellied stove. "You can keep your snow and your white Christmas. I'm happy right where I am."

"You'd be happy anywhere as long as Jack was there, and you know it."

A shy smile twisted the corners of Maggie's mouth, and color bloomed in her cheeks. "Well, maybe."

"Maybe, my foot." Annabelle grinned and bumped her shoulder against Maggie's.

Soon the church emptied, and Annabelle helped her mother gather up the little ones as her father brought the wagon around.

"Maggie, I hope you'll join us for dinner." Annabelle's mother tossed the invitation over her shoulder as she herded her brood out the door. "Samuel, that goes for you, too."

"What about me?" Jack called out as he closed the damper on the woodstove.

"I couldn't beat you off with a stick, Jack, so I guess that means you're invited."

"Maggie, see how my own mother treats me." Jack threw a hand to his chest and staggered back as if mortally wounded. The children giggled at their older brother's antics.

Annabelle caught Maggie's attention, raised her eyebrows, and nodded toward her brother. "That is what you have to look forward to."

Her friend just smiled, and they all trooped outside. Jack sidled up to Maggie and whispered, "Walk with me?"

She blushed and nodded. Jack snagged Annabelle's arm. "You, too, sis."

"Walk? Have you lost your mind?" Annabelle sputtered, and made a half-hearted attempt to pull free, knowing full well that Jack only wanted her along as chaperone. "It's too cold to walk. And besides, I need to help Mama put dinner on the table."

"Sally can help until you get there." Her mother's lips twitched as her gaze landed pointedly on Jack. "Don't dally, now. You hear?"

"Yes ma'am."

The wagon rattled off toward home, and Annabelle and Samuel fell into step together, Jack and Maggie bringing up the rear. As the distance between the two couples widened, Annabelle pursed her lips. "I think we've been hornswoggled."

A tiny smiled kicked up one side of Samuel's mouth, and he stuffed his hands in his coat pockets and sauntered along like he didn't have a care in the world. "How's that?"

Annabelle huffed. "We're walking along this muddy, wagon-wheel-gutted road—in the wind, mind you—so that those two lovebirds can get all flutterpated."

Samuel laughed. "It's hard for them to get any time alone, and they needed a chaperone."

"Well, they could wait till spring."

"They might not have until spring."

"What's that supposed to mean?"

"Maggie's pa is talking about heading west."

"Oh." Annabelle pulled her coat closer to ward off the chill. No wonder Jack wanted to spend as much time with Maggie as he could. The scripture about contentment flitted across her mind. Why couldn't Maggie's pa be content wherever he was? It wasn't like he didn't have good Christian neighbors, plenty of food, and a homestead any man would be proud of. His oldest daughter certainly didn't want to leave Sipsey, and her mother and younger siblings seemed happy as well. Maybe he didn't think that being content in whatsoever state he was in meant in the state of Mississippi.

They walked a bit farther, the wind cutting through Annabelle's woolen scarf. She shuddered.

"Cold?" Samuel asked.

"Yes. That wind cuts right through me."

"It's going to be a lot colder in Illinois."

"Maybe, but it's a different kind of cold. Or at least that's what Lucy says."

"Cold is cold to my way of thinking."

"But the snow will make it worth it."

Maggie's soft giggle floated to them on the brisk

wind. Annabelle glanced back and saw her brother pulling Maggie close to his side. She tapped Samuel's arm. "Look. Some chaperones we're turning out to be." She turned around, walking backward, and called out, "Hey, you two, stop that."

Jack shot her a look that would melt snow faster than a bonfire at a sing-along.

Samuel reached out, snaked an arm around her waist, and lifted her off the ground. "Leave 'em alone. They deserve a bit of privacy."

"Put me down, you big oaf." Laughing, Annabelle squirmed, plucking at his coat sleeve, knowing the effort was futile. Samuel's arms were like bands of steel around her waist, and he'd put her down when he was good and ready.

He let her go, his brown eyes laughing. Her feet on firm ground once again, she attempted to peek at Jack and Maggie. Samuel took a step toward her. "Don't even think about it."

She laughed and let him have his way. They passed the sawmill, the weathered building still and silent on a Sunday. No welcoming smoke rose from the chimney like it did on weekdays when Samuel and Jack were there, the warmth a welcome break halfway between the school and home. Annabelle frowned, her thoughtful gaze on the small barn-like structure tucked in a clearing away from prying eyes. "Sometimes I wonder about propriety."

Samuel lifted a brow and grunted. Clearly, he had no idea what she was talking about.

"Take those two back there. They've been courting for two years now. Why is it that society still expects them to have a chaperone?"

"Because they're courting."

"But that's just it. People should expect them to want to spend some time together."

"But not alone." Samuel shook his head. "They should never, ever be alone."

"Aha." Annabelle turned around and walked backward, enjoying the banter, and knowing she had him trapped. "They're alone now. Maybe we should wait."

"They'll be along shortly." Samuel gave her a lopsided smile. "Turn around."

She grinned at him, still trying to walk backward and carry on a conversation at the same time. "Nobody thinks anything about it when I stop at the sawmill. Why is that?"

A funny expression crossed Samuel's face, and she laughed. "What? What did I say?"

"Nothing." He shook his head, a half-smile turning

up the corners of his mouth, as if the topic amused him. She made a note to tell Lucy what a nice smile he had.

The heel of her boot caught on a wagon wheel rut, and she stumbled. Samuel grabbed her just before she fell flat on her back in the muddy road. As he held her close, the lingering scent of bay rum tickled her nose. She lifted her gaze to meet his, a teasing remark about her clumsiness on the tip of her tongue.

But when their eyes met, she froze, suspended for a moment in time. She'd never seen Samuel's eyes quite this close. They were brown, with flecks of gold. Mesmerized, she wondered why she'd never noticed that before. His gaze flickered, then lowered, sweeping across her face before settling on her lips.

"Hey, you two, stop that."

At the sound of Jack's teasing laughter, Samuel set her on her feet and let her go. Annabelle concentrated on her footing, all thoughts of teasing and laughter completely forgotten as she willed her heart rate to slow to normal.

One near fall today was enough, thank you very much.

Chapter 5

Samuel stuffed his hands in his pockets, heart pounding like a runaway mule. What just happened? One minute they'd been walking along, Annabelle teasing him with silly questions about propriety and courting and such, then the next minute she'd been in his arms.

If Jack and Maggie hadn't rounded the bend, he would have kissed her for sure.

What had come over him?

Annabelle had.

Her laughing green eyes and soft, silky hair that smelled like roses in springtime; her willowy frame that no amount of layered winter coats could disguise.

He chanced a glance at her, walking two steps ahead and to his right, her scarf blocking her face from his view. Had she realized what had almost transpired? Surely she had. He wanted to kick himself. He hadn't meant to let his feelings be known so soon. Not with her about to leave for Illinois.

The Denson homestead came into view, and Annabelle's little brother Ike raced out the door and launched himself at Samuel. Samuel hoisted the boy high, grateful for the distraction. He held the door open as he'd done more times than he could count, but this time Annabelle's gaze ricocheted off his and she murmured thank you before hurrying inside.

Little Ike wrapped his arms around Samuel's neck and squeezed tight, but not as tight as the vice wrapped around his chest. Had Annabelle been distracted by the need to help her mother with dinner, or had his actions caused her to avoid him?

Mrs. Denson's Sunday dinner was as good as ever, but Samuel's stomach was too tied up in knots to enjoy it. Seated between Ike and Ander, he teased the boys and concentrated on eating, simply because it kept his mind off Annabelle. He couldn't bear to see the confusion in her eyes, on her face. The conversation centered around the sawmill equipment he and Samuel planned to get from Abe Jensen.

"What do you think, Pa?" Jack asked before shoveling a helping of field peas in his mouth, followed by a generous bite of cornbread.

"Abe Jenson is a good businessman, and he's looking to make some money. He wouldn't bother if he didn't think the old engine still had some life in her." Reverend Denson nodded, considering the offer. "If you boys can get her to run, I think it's a fair offer."

A weight lifted off Samuel's shoulders. He valued Reverend Denson's opinion. "We'll need to make several trips."

"I'll hook up the wagon tomorrow and go along with you."

Jack grinned. "Thanks, Pa. We could sure use the help."

The conversation turned to Annabelle's trip, with Maggie peppering Annabelle with questions and Sally begging her mother to let her go to Illinois with her sister. Samuel didn't join in the conversation, unwilling to risk letting anyone know how he really felt about Annabelle leaving.

"Are you going to the Art Institute?" Maggie asked.

"Yes, if the weather permits. And to the library. Lucy says there are two, the Newberry Library and the Chicago Public Library. Can you imagine all those books in one place?"

"Are you going to any Christmas balls?" Sally piped up.

"I don't think your aunt and uncle know anybody that would hold a ball, Sally." Mrs. Denson nodded at Sally's plate. "Eat your peas if you want some dessert."

"You gonna eat that pie?" Jack stabbed a

fork at Samuel's plate.

"Get away." Samuel braced his forearms on each side of his dessert plate and pushed Jack's fork away. "Eat your own pie."

"Well, I was just wondering. You've been staring at it for half an hour. Pa's sermon get to you this morning?"

"Something like that." Samuel shoved a forkful of pie into his mouth and chewed, hoping Jack would take his answer for fact, and leave him be.

For the first time ever, Mrs. Denson's hot apple pie with its flaky crust stuck in his throat like he'd inhaled a mouthful of sawdust.

Chapter 6

Sunday evening worship and chores done, Annabelle took her writing supplies from her hope chest. She had just enough time to pen a letter to Lucy before bedtime. She peeked into the sitting room on her way to the kitchen, the warmest—and the *quietest*—room in her parents' drafty old house.

Her mother darned socks while her pa dozed and rocked Lilly, humming under his breath. Her little brothers played with the wooden logs and toy soldiers Samuel had carved for them.

Samuel.

Annabelle's heart lurched. She'd managed to push thoughts of today to the back of her mind, what with helping her mother clean up after Sunday dinner, evening chores, and family worship right after supper.

But now, in the quiet before bed, it all came rushing back.

She sank into a chair at the kitchen table and untied the ribbon that held her writing supplies, the events of today's almost-kiss flooding her thoughts.

What would it be like to be kissed? By *Samuel* even? She'd imagined her first kiss, and a few times she'd tried to picture her first beau, but never in a million years had she imagined being held securely in Samuel's strong arms, his gaze capturing her lips.

Samuel kissing her.

Samuel even *wanting* to kiss her.

Maybe she'd read too much into the thud of his heart as he held her, his face so close to hers, his gaze drifting down and settling on her lips. Cheeks flaming, she flipped open her leather writing satchel. She'd do well not to dwell on what had happened today. Samuel had eaten his dinner as usual, accepted Jack's teasing with a crooked smile, defended his dessert, but for the most part, remained quiet.

Just like always.

He hadn't acted as if anything out of the ordinary had transpired. But she'd been so flustered by her own reaction to being held in his arms that she'd avoided looking at him. She pulled out a piece of paper and found her pencil, teeth worrying her bottom lip.

What if he had tried to catch her eye during Sunday dinner? Their gazes had met and held for a moment when the men were discussing business. And his expression hadn't held even a hint that the incident on the road had meant anything to him. Clearly, she'd blown the whole thing out of proportion, when he'd already forgotten it. Just because she'd glimpsed one of those crooked little smiles of his as he held her close didn't mean a thing. For heaven's sake, she might have had mud on her face or a smudge of soot, and he'd been laughing at her as usual. If Jack hadn't yelled out about that time, Samuel would have made some teasing remark about her clumsiness.

She sighed. All would be back to normal when she returned from her trip to Illinois.

Is that what you want?

Annabelle blinked, staring at the blank paper. Except the stationery was no longer blank. Sweeping swirls of romantic doodles covered the page. Hearts and flowers and curling garnishes surrounded the name *Samuel*, penned dreamily in her very own flowing, fanciful hand.

Chapter 7

"Matt, put that peashooter away this instant."

Several boys giggled, and Matt grinned. "Sorry, Annabelle, I was just showing it to Ander."

"*Miss* Annabelle." Annabelle glared at him, knowing full well he'd been doing more than just showing his new peashooter to her brother. Why on earth had she ever thought she could teach children who'd known her all their lives? Papa had put the fear into her three siblings, and they behaved well enough, but sometimes she had trouble keeping the rest of them in line.

Of course, the youngest ones adored her and applied themselves to their lessons with gusto. It was the children who'd been in school when she graduated that caused the most problems. They had a hard time separating the Annabelle they'd gone to school with from Miss Annabelle, the teacher. When she'd agreed to take on this task, she hadn't realized how difficult it would be to teach in her own community. She'd stick it out until school dismissed for the summer then see about transferring somewhere else.

Matt stuffed the peashooter into his pocket and grinned at Sally. Sally concentrated on her ciphering, as if she didn't have a care in the world. But Annabelle had seen the spitball land in Sally's hair. She shook her head. Why Matt thought shooting spitballs at Sally would get her sister's attention was beyond her. But she remembered being that age and Amos Rosenthal doing the same thing. Well, it had certainly earned him her attention, but not necessarily in a good way.

The clock said they had thirty more minutes, and then she could let the children go for the day. They'd become more and more restless as Christmas drew near, and she had a feeling this last week was going to be trying for all of them.

"Let's continue. Matt, start up where Beth left off."

Matt groaned, but did as he was told. "Johnny Reed was a li–lit. . ."

"Little."

"Little boy who ne–ne–ver had seen a sn–snow. . ."

"Snowstorm."

"Snowstorm, um. . .until he was six years old. Be–before this he had l–lived in. . ."

The back door opened, and Matt trailed off. Maggie stuck her head in, eyebrows lifted as if asking permission to enter. A ripple of excitement wafted over the students at the intrusion. Visitors at school were few and far between, and Annabelle knew she'd lost their attention for the day. She closed her book, and Matt sat up straight, a grin splitting his face. She gave him what she hoped was a stern look.

"All right, children. Gather your things. I think we can leave a few minutes early today. Sally, you may ring the bell."

Pandemonium erupted and within minutes, the children had donned coats, gloves, and hats, and scattered for the door, whooping and hollering.

Maggie flattened herself against the wall, out of the way. "My goodness, what a stampede."

"You don't want to be caught in their path at the end of the day, that's for sure."

"I'll say." Her friend watched as Annabelle closed the damper on the woodstove and straightened the papers on her desk. "Sometimes I envy you."

"Me?" Annabelle lifted an eyebrow, surprised. "What in the world for?"

"You get to experience something new and exciting every day, while my life is the same thing day after day out on the farm." Maggie toyed with a paperweight on Annabelle's desk. "Well, except today. Today was different. I helped Pa shell corn and haul it to the gristmill."

"Oh, so that's why you stopped by today. You've been to the gristmill."

"Pa went on without me. I asked him to drop me off and pick me up at your house on his way home." Maggie followed Annabelle to the door. "I hope you don't mind?"

"Of course not." Annabelle reached for her coat. "I don't get to see you often enough."

Maggie looked away, but not before Annabelle saw the tears in her eyes. "Maggie? What's wrong? Is your pa talking about heading west again?"

"It's all he talks about." She blinked back the tears and sniffed. "Annabelle, I don't know if I can bear to leave Jack."

"If I know my brother, he'll find a way to keep you here."

Color bloomed on Maggie's face, and she whispered, "But he hasn't asked me yet."

"Asked you what?"

"To marry him. Do you. . .do you think he loves me? Enough to want to marry me?"

"I do." Annabelle hugged her, then held her at arm's length. "Who knows why he hasn't asked you yet? He could be waiting until Christmas, or he could just think you already know what he wants."

"How would I know that?"

Annabelle gathered up a stack of books and handed them to Maggie. "Because, my friend, he expects you to read his mind."

"I'll never understand men."

"Me neither." Annabelle locked the door, joined Maggie at the bottom of the porch stairs, and linked arms with her friend. "And I certainly don't understand my brother."

Their laughter lightened the mood as they headed toward home, and Annabelle was grateful for Maggie's assistance with the books and papers she had to carry as well as more than a little grateful for the company. With Maggie along, the decision on whether to stop at the sawmill was out of her hands. Of course Maggie would want to stop and see Jack.

More than once today, she'd wrestled with whether she should drop in as usual or just walk on by. Knowing that she hadn't quite put yesterday's incident behind her, she didn't know if she could pretend nothing had happened if she found Samuel alone.

Her face flamed. With her newfound awareness of him, she knew now why a chaperone was necessary for her brother and Maggie. Goodness, she'd been tempted to ask Sally to stay after school and walk with her just so she'd have an excuse not to stop.

But she hadn't said anything. Because truth be told, she wanted to see Samuel.

Chapter 8

"Just my luck."

Jack's outburst barely registered as Samuel adjusted the tension on the belt that powered the saw blade. He knew a bit about steam engines from working with Abe. He just hoped he knew enough to get this one up and running without blowing them to smithereens.

"Are you listening?" Jack waved a piece of paper in front of Samuel's face. "Maggie and Annabelle stopped by yesterday while we were gone to Abe's."

Mention of Annabelle pulled Samuel's thoughts from the work set before him. He'd wondered if she'd come after what happened Sunday, but it couldn't be helped that he'd missed her. It had taken most of the afternoon to dismantle the machinery at Abe's and load everything in the wagons. They hadn't made it back until nearly dark.

He frowned. Maggie? "What was Maggie doing with her? Is something wrong?"

"No. She stopped off to visit Annabelle at the school while her pa went to the gristmill." Jack stuffed the note in his pocket. "She said she had something important to tell me, but didn't want to put it in writing."

"Do you think it might be about her pa's itch to move on?"

"What else could it be?" Jack scowled.

Samuel didn't answer. Since the threat of separation hung over Jack and Maggie, Jack was probably right. What encouragement could he offer? None, but he could keep his friend busy. He gave the steam engine a pat. "Let's give this saw a run."

The chug-chug of the engine and the whir of the blade filled the air, and Samuel's heart sang along as he and Jack tested out the blade. They debarked a log then eased it through the blade. Sawdust flew in every direction, but they concentrated on the task at hand as the blade sliced into their very first board.

Jack grinned at their handiwork. "I know exactly where I'm going to use this."

Samuel quirked a brow. "Where?"

"Over the front door."

"One board does not a house make." Samuel nodded toward the block of wood as they readied it for another pass. "Steady now."

As the afternoon wore on, Jack and Samuel realized just how temperamental the old steam engine was, and how exhausting hefting logs onto the ramp and rolling them in to position could be. Midafternoon, the blade jerked, lodging itself against the log, and the belt started spinning.

Heart pounding, Samuel scrambled to kill the power to the engine before something blew. As he and Jack tinkered with the cantankerous old equipment, their early excitement waned.

"I'm not sure if this is worth it." Jack wiped his brow and took a long swig of water from a canning jar. He wiped his mouth on his sleeve. "At this rate, we'd be better off hauling logs to Abe just like we've been doing."

Samuel searched for the problem, determined not to give up so easily. His heart sank when he saw that one of the braces that held the blade straight and true had cracked. He pointed. "Look."

"Piece of junk. No wonder Abe wanted to get rid of it."

"It's not so bad. If we can get this piece off, Zeke might be able to forge it back together."

An hour later, Jack headed to the blacksmith's with the iron bar in hand, and Samuel eyed the saw blade wedged against the log, trying to decide the best course of action. The one thing he didn't want to do was ruin that blade, or Jack's dream of building a house and a life with Maggie would be even further out of reach.

He loosened the belt that provided traction for the blade but the blade held fast, wedged tight against the unforgiving pine log. Nothing for it. He grabbed a saw. Better to waste part of the log than ruin their only blade.

He'd worked up a sweat by the time he sawed away the board and the blade jerked back into alignment. *Lord, please don't let any of these teeth be chipped.*

A rain of sawdust fell on his head, and he looked up to see Annabelle smiling at him, her cheeks glowing from the cold. His heart rate spiked at the sight of her. She slapped her gloved hands together, and sawdust fluttered on the slight breeze and peppered her coat and scarf, reminding him of the snow she longed to see in Illinois. A smile wreathed her face. "You got the saw to work!"

"Well, yes and no."

Her smile slipped. "No?"

"It worked fine until a piece broke." He showed her where the broken brace had been.

She moved closer and peered at the spot. "Oh, no. Can it be fixed?"

"Maybe." Samuel shoved his hat back. "Jack

took it to Zeke."

"That's good. Zeke should be able to make it good as new."

The breeze blew her soft floral scent toward him, and he swallowed, trying not to think about how she'd felt in his arms on Sunday. How her lips had softened and parted just before Jack had called out. He pulled his gaze from her face and settled on the multi-colored scarf covering her hair. "You're covered in sawdust."

"Uh oh." She brushed at the flecks clinging to her scarf. "That won't be easy to get out."

"Reminds me of snow."

"It does, doesn't it?"

He couldn't resist her laugh, and found himself looking into her eyes again. Did she feel the electric charge in the air? A charge he'd managed to keep buried deep down inside.

At least until last Sunday.

She cleared her throat and moved away. "I got another letter from Lucy. She said that it started snowing, and they've already put sled runners on the wagons. Did you know that? I never really thought about it, since we've never had any need for sled runners here in Mississippi. And there's going to be a Christmas play at her church, and her pastor's wife invited us to dinner one night. She said we could go sledding, and ice skating—that is, if the ice on the pond is thick enough. She said everybody comes out on Saturday afternoon to skate since it's not every year that they get the chance."

Samuel watched the emotions playing across Annabelle's face as she prattled on and on about all the things she'd do and see in Illinois. Her eyes danced with excitement, and her cheeks bloomed with color that didn't have anything to do with the slight chill in the air.

"What?" Annabelle gave him a tentative smile, and he realized she'd stopped talking about Illinois and was staring at him.

He said the first thing that popped into his head. "With so much to do, you're liable to end up staying in Illinois."

"Oh, no, I can't imagine that happening." She laughed, a bit shakily, before looking away and picking up the canning jar Jack had left sitting on the windowsill, sawdust settling in the water. "I mean, what would I do there?"

Samuel's heart slammed against his ribcage as the truth hit him. She had considered moving to Illinois. Why hadn't he seen it?

She shook the jar, and the tiny flecks of wood swirled in the water. She lifted her gaze, all trace of teasing and laughter gone. Her eyes, the exact color of the pines towering behind her, met his briefly before she looked away and gathered up her school satchel. "I'd better go. I hope you and Jack get the saw going again."

Long after she'd gone, Samuel turned the conversation over in his mind. What if she met someone in Illinois? She was smart and beautiful and would make some man a good wife. There'd be any number of men who'd want to court her, and he'd given her no reason to come back to Mississippi.

What a fool he'd been.

Pride in having enough to provide for a wife and family had kept him from making the slightest move to let Annabelle know how he felt. He needed to do something, say something before she left to let her know that he cared. That he wanted her to come back.

His gaze landed on the canning jar half full of water, the sawdust swirling slower and slower, until it gradually began to sink to the bottom like softly falling flakes of snow. He reached out, lifted the jar, and gave it a gentle shake as an idea began to form.

Chapter 9

Samuel pictured the carving in his mind as he turned the block of wood in his hand. The entire carving wouldn't be much bigger than the palm of his hand, and the details would be small and delicate. He itched to be out in the woods felling timber, but falling temperatures and a steady rain earlier in the day had kept them from the woods. Even so, the time hadn't been wasted. It had taken two days for Zeke to fix the brace on the engine, and Samuel and Jack had cut up the rest of the logs small enough to run through the saw blade.

He chuckled. Actually, they'd cut up anything and everything that even looked like it could be used in Jack's house. They were a long way from having enough lumber, but that hadn't stopped Jack from sketching his dream house out on paper.

"What do you think about this?"

Samuel paused in his carving and eyed the crude drawing Jack had made. He pointed with his knife. "I'd put a door right there, off the main room. That'll make it easy to add on an extra room when you need it."

"Good idea." Jack nodded toward the block of wood as he scratched in a door with his snubby-nosed pencil. "What are you making?"

Samuel hefted the three-sided carving, the image of their small country church beginning to take shape on one side. "Christmas present for Annabelle."

"She's not going to be here for Christmas."

"I know."

Jack laughed, still fiddling with his plans. Suddenly, his pencil poised in midair, he squinted at Samuel, an odd look on his face. "You sweet on my sister?"

Samuel didn't see any sense in denying it. He nodded toward the open sawmill doors. "It's stopped raining. Maybe you should hook up the mules and head on in to town with that load of logs."

Jack ignored him. "I should have noticed before now, I guess. She doesn't stop by here every day to see me."

"Sure she does."

"What about last Sunday?"

"She tripped and I caught her. That's all."

Jack crossed his arms over his chest, the worn fabric of his work shirt stretched tight. "Looked like more than that to me."

Samuel gritted his teeth. It was more. A lot more.

But Jack didn't need to know that. "It wasn't."

Jack snorted. "When are you going to tell her how you feel?"

Samuel sighed. There was no use trying to deny that he had feelings for Annabelle. "I'm not."

"Why not? She's going to Illinois next week."

"And that's why I'm not going to say anything. She's got her heart set on a white Christmas, and I won't do anything to ruin it for her."

Jack stretched and reached for his hat. "You just keep thinking like that, buddy, and she's liable to meet some yahoo up in Illinois, and then where will you be?"

After Jack left, Samuel stared at the block of wood where he carved his hopes and dreams for the future. Would it be enough? Enough to bring Annabelle back to him?

Chapter 10

Weary from a long day of teaching, Annabelle locked the schoolhouse, thankful for the Christmas break that gave her three glorious weeks of freedom. It had been all she could do to keep the children under control all week but practically impossible today, they'd been so excited.

From the schoolhouse steps, she stood on tiptoe and squinted through the cloudy midwinter haze. She could barely see Miller's Mercantile at the crossroads on the other side of the church. Sipsey couldn't even be called a town unless you counted the church and the school, along with Mr. Miller's store, and you couldn't always count the store.

The tiny mercantile consisted of two wagons butted end to end. The space was so tight, you just entered from one end and exited the other, and every nook and cranny was stuffed full of nonperishables, spices, sundry items, and a bit of cloth and thread. Mr. Miller moved his store to a new location whenever the mood struck him. She hurried toward the wagons, thankful he hadn't packed up and moved today. Regardless of the lateness of the hour, her mother had asked her to pick up some salt, and with school out, she didn't know when she'd have another chance to stop in.

In no time at all, she made her purchases and headed toward home, carefully avoiding the puddles left by the recent rain. Free of trying to corral a dozen children, the fluttery feeling of anticipation she'd become familiar with this week niggled at her the closer she got to the sawmill.

When she'd stopped by the last two days, Zeke, Jack, and Samuel had been up to their eyeballs trying to get the old steam engine running. With her brother and the crotchety old blacksmith there, it had been easy to make small talk for a few minutes before heading on home.

On one hand, she'd been relieved not to find Samuel alone, since the opportunity to see him without having to talk put her at ease over Sunday's episode, but on the other, she'd been disappointed. Which would have seemed downright silly a week ago. But today, the feeling was anything but silly or trivial.

In the distance, she spotted a wisp of smoke curling above the tops of the pine trees. She rounded the last bend, and her gaze swept the familiar weathered boards of the barn-like structure, the lean-to on the left that housed the steam engine, the barn and pasture out back. Zeke's wagon, with all his scraps of iron, was nowhere to be seen, but the fresh pile of cut lumber stacked under the lean-to was testament that they'd gotten the saw going again. And the big freight wagon Samuel and Jack used to transport logs to town was gone.

Her steps faltered, and her heart skittered. Was Samuel here? Or Jack? Had they both gone to deliver logs? Should she stop in or not? The lure of the wood-stove's warmth drew her, and she hurried toward the doors pulled shut against the cold.

She pushed one of the huge doors open just enough to slip inside. Disappointment filled her as she realized the room was empty. She'd convinced herself that she hadn't longed to see Samuel, that her concern was just for their business and her brother and Maggie's plans for the future.

Well, nothing for it. Jack was gone, and so was Samuel. A pot of coffee sat on the stove. Ah, coffee. She sniffed and closed her eyes in appreciation. Just what she needed to warm her for the walk home. She removed her gloves, snagged a cup from one of the pegs, and poured, then sat on the stool next to the stove. As she sipped the brew—a bit bitter, but not too bad—her gaze landed on Samuel's tools and the partially carved train set spread across the table. Probably a Christmas present for one of her brothers. She leaned closer to inspect one of the boxcars, complete with working wheels and tiny axles fashioned from nails.

The door creaked open and she jumped, almost spilling her coffee. Samuel entered, a load of firewood in his arms. He turned, eyes widening at the sight of her before a slight smile turned up the corners of his mouth. "I'd given up on you today."

He'd been watching for her?

Warmth filled her, and it had nothing to do with the coffee. "I had to run to Miller's Mercantile for a few things."

"Still at the crossroads, then?" He took off his coat and hung it on a peg by the door.

"Still there. But not for long. He said to tell everybody that he's thinking of moving to Kitchener next week, so if you need anything, you'd better get it now."

"He says that every Christmas."

"True."

He opened the firebox and poked at the burning embers. Sparks flew, illuminating a days-old shadow on his cheeks, a shadow that he'd shave off come

Sunday morning. She studied his profile underneath the brim of his hat. He tossed a couple of sticks of wood into the firebox and threw her a glance, his dark eyes reflecting the flames. "That should warm you up for the trip home."

Annabelle laughed. "Are you trying to get rid of me already?"

"Nope. You're welcome to stay as long as you want." A tiny smile kicked up one side of his mouth again. His shirt stretched taut across his shoulders as he reached for the coffeepot. "More coffee?"

"No, thank you." Annabelle quelled the flutter in her stomach. Heart pounding, she lowered her gaze and stared into her coffee cup. What was wrong with her? When had she become so aware of every move Samuel made? Since Sunday, when she'd tripped and somehow got it into her head that he'd wanted to kiss her, that's when. She'd wrestled with questioning him about it all week. But what could she say?

Were you going to kiss me?

No, she couldn't. She wouldn't ask him such a question. Her cheeks flamed as she tried to think of a way to broach the subject without embarrassing either of them.

A jingle of harness alerted her that Jack had

returned. She placed the cup on the table and stood, panic at what she'd almost said mingled with a wild desire to know the answer to the question that had kept her awake five nights in a row. "I'd better get home."

"I'll take you in the wagon."

"No, that's not necessary."

"It'll be dark soon, and the temperature is dropping." He moved to the door and called out, "Hey, Jack, just leave 'em hitched. I'm going to take Annabelle home."

Thankful that she didn't have to walk the rest of the way home after today's rain, Annabelle headed outside. Her brother grumbled good-naturedly as he set the brake and jumped down, grinning at her. "What's the matter, sis? Afraid you'll get a little mud on ya?"

"You know good and well I'm not afraid of a little mud, Jack Denson."

Samuel climbed into the tall freight wagon then reached for Annabelle's hand as Jack hoisted her up. Her brother winked up at her. "Y'all have fun. Straight there and back, now, you hear?"

The ride home took less than ten minutes, but Annabelle was too mortified to even look at Samuel. Jack acted like she and Samuel were courting, for heaven's sake, and Samuel hadn't even said one word to her that would make her think he was interested.

Samuel reined in the mules, set the brake, and jumped down, only to be swarmed by Ike and Ander running out to meet them. Annabelle eyed the distance to the ground from the lowest rung on the wagon. She clambered over the side before Samuel could untangle himself, only to find herself a good foot or more off the ground, with no foothold.

Samuel glanced at her, her little brothers dangling from his arms. "Need help?"

"Well, it seems I do. There's no way to get down."

"Sorry. This wagon wasn't built for ladies." He shooed her brothers away and moved closer. His hands encircled her waist, and even though she could barely feel his touch through the bulk of her coat, her heart fluttered. Her hands landed on his shoulders and he lowered her to the ground, so close, she could see the golden flecks in his brown eyes. Not a trace of laughter lingered in their depths. "It wouldn't do for you to fall right before your trip to Illinois."

"Like last time?" she blurted out, regretting the question immediately. If he didn't remember, or made some teasing remark about her clumsiness, then she'd know the event meant nothing to him.

His gaze softened, dipped, and settled on her mouth before flicking to meet hers again. "Like last time."

Chapter 11

The sun barely peeked over the horizon, and Annabelle looked around her room, trying to determine what she'd missed. Two bags sat beside the door, and she mentally ticked off the contents carefully folded and stuffed inside. She couldn't think of a thing she'd forgotten.

Then why did she feel so unsettled? *Discontented*, even.

Guilt stabbed her. She'd brushed off Maggie's father's desire to uproot his family as discontentment. Did she harbor a bit of unhappiness in her own heart? A longing for change for the sake of change, regardless of whether it was for the better or even good for her?

She plopped down on the bed and stared out the window. Where had the excitement over her trip gone? For as long as she could remember, she'd dreamed of a white Christmas. Every year, without fail, it was the one thing she'd wished for. Oh, there'd been a little snow here and there, but nothing to compare with what her cousin described. Surely the desire for one short trip wasn't the sign of a discontented heart.

She lifted the lid of her hope chest, just to be sure she hadn't forgotten anything. As she riffled through pillowcases, dishes, and hand towels embroidered with snowflakes against a background of evergreens, and all the other things a young woman stored away in anticipation of the day she'd set up housekeeping in her own home, she finally admitted to herself what was bothering her.

What she'd left undone.

Unbeknownst to anyone, other than maybe to Lucy, Annabelle's dream of a white Christmas was just a small part of her trip. She dreamed of finally meeting the one man who could make her heart sing, the one man who would look at her with stars in his eyes and who'd say sweet things to her, bring her wildflowers in the springtime. The one man who would tell her he couldn't live without her. She'd thought she'd find that man in Illinois. But what if he was right here, here in Mississippi, underneath the pines?

What if Samuel is that man?

But she didn't know how he felt. Did he even think about her like she'd begun to think about him? He'd wished her well on her trip and teased her about coming back. But he hadn't given any indication that he might care for her in any way other than as his partner's sister and as a friend.

A light knock sounded on the door, and Annabelle's mother poked her head in, a smile on her face. "You ready for your big adventure?"

"I can't believe it's finally here." Annabelle smiled, struggling to push thoughts of Samuel to the back of her mind.

"Enjoy it. Two weeks will go faster than you ever dreamed." Her mother hugged her and held her at arm's length. "Now, you be good, mind your manners, and don't go off alone with any young man, no matter how respectable your aunt claims he is."

"Mama, you know I'd never. . ."

"I know, but it's a mama's duty to issue these warnings. And I just don't trust those big-city boys, not by a long shot." She reached for a soft-sided carpetbag. "Now, gather your things. Jack's downstairs and rarin' to go."

"Jack?" Annabelle grabbed the other bag and followed her mother down the hall. "I thought Papa was taking us to the train station."

"He got called away. Old Mr. Hedricks is in a bad way and asked for him. Your pa asked Jack to take you and your aunt to the train station."

"Oh no. Is Mr. Hedricks going to be all right?"

"Don't worry now. Just his stomach ulcers giving him fits. I'm sure he'll be fine." They hurried outside, and Jack put her bags in the wagon bed. Her mother shaded her eyes and glanced at the sky. "Thank goodness it's not raining today, or you'd have to take Eugenia's buggy."

"Knowing Aunt Eugenia, we might have to anyway." Jack helped Annabelle into the wagon and climbed up beside her.

"Well, get on then. You don't want to be late. Mind what I told you, Annabelle."

"Yes ma'am."

Jack slapped the reins against the horses' flanks and they headed out. A package slid along the seat, and Annabelle grabbed it to keep it from falling. "What's this?"

"Oh, Samuel sent that. Said to give it to you and that you weren't to open it until Christmas morning."

"Really? How sweet." Annabelle ran the tips of her fingers over the odd-shaped package wrapped in plain brown wrapping paper and tied with a string. Her heart fluttered. How could she wait another week to see what Samuel had gotten her?

Her brother scowled. "Samuel? Sweet?"

"Of course he's sweet."

Jack rested his elbows on his knees, the reins clasped between his fingers. "Then why are you gallivanting off to Illinois chasing after some beau if you think my partner is *sweet?*"

"I'm *not* chasing off after a beau." Annabelle glared at her brother, then shrugged. "You know I just want a white Christmas."

He arched a brow at her. "So you're saying that you won't even look at a man while you're there? That you and Lucy haven't talked about men in all those letters y'all have sent back and forth, back and forth, day after day? Nobody can write that much about snow and dresses and such nonsense."

Annabelle squirmed. "Well, Lucy might have mentioned a few fellows that she wants me to meet."

Jack grinned. "See, I told you."

"But it doesn't mean a thing."

"Just like you calling Samuel sweet doesn't mean a thing either?" He nodded at the package. "Or him taking the time to make you a present, knowing you weren't even going to be here for Christmas."

"He made it?"

Her brother grimaced. "I wasn't supposed to tell you that part."

Annabelle fingered the string. What could it be? Something made from wood, no doubt. A small box for trinkets and ribbons? A carving of some kind? Smoke from the mill curled above the treetops around the next bend. She needed to thank Samuel. His was the only present she was taking from home.

As they rounded the bend, and the mill came into view, Annabelle put a hand on her brother's arm. "Stop."

"No time." Jack didn't slack up. "Aunt Eugenia's waiting."

"Jack. Please." Annabelle held up the package. "I can't leave without thanking him."

Chapter 12

Samuel had kept himself busy from the moment Reverend Denson had stopped by to ask Jack to drive Annabelle and Miss Eugenia into town. Jack would be gone most of the day, so they wouldn't be able to cut any logs, but he could finish up the last of his projects for Christmas, starting with the rocking chair for Mrs. Denson.

The reverend wanted him to deliver it bright and early Christmas morning, and had even invited him to stay for dinner, but Samuel wouldn't be eating Christmas dinner with the Densons this year. He couldn't stomach the thought of sitting there listening to the family's laughter with Annabelle's empty chair across from him.

He sanded the chair runners, the scraping filling the quietness of the shop.

"Samuel?"

His stomach did a slow roll at the unexpected sound of Annabelle's soft voice. Turning, he saw her silhouetted in the open doorway, in a dark green dress that brought out the color of her eyes, and her best Sunday coat and scarf.

"What are you doing here?" He smiled to take the sting out of his blunt question. "Don't you have a train to catch?"

"We're on the way now." She glided across the sawdust-strewn floor, her eyes sparkling. "But I couldn't leave without thanking you for the gift."

"It's not much." He shrugged, his heart rate kicking up a notch when she rested a hand on his arm.

"It is to me. It'll be the only present from home that I'll have to open on Christmas morning." Her smile slipped, and she blinked, a hint of moisture spiking her lashes.

"Hey, what's this?" Samuel dipped his head and peered into her face. "Tears just before your grand adventure?"

"Silly, isn't it?" She shook her head and sniffed. "I know you told me already, but it just hit me that this will be the first time in my life that I'll be away from my family during Christmas."

"Well, it's just for two weeks, and you'll be back." *Lord, please let her come back.* "If you don't go off and forget about us."

"I won't." She shook her head. "Thank you for the present, Samuel. No matter what it is, I'll treasure it for always." She raised on tiptoe and kissed his cheek. Her gaze searched his, and it was all he could do not to tell her that he loved her, that he didn't want her to go.

"Annabelle!" Jack called from outside. "Hurry up. Time's a wastin'."

Something akin to disappointment shuttered her features, and she turned away. Samuel could no more stop himself than he could stop the train carrying her away from him. He reached out and lightly clasped her slender wrist. At his touch, her lashes swept up and her eyes met his, a question in their depths.

He tugged, and she came willingly. She closed her eyes and tilted her face up to meet his kiss, and her lips were as sweet and tender as he'd dreamed they would be. The kiss lasted seconds, or minutes, he was never sure, but one thing he was sure of, it wasn't long enough.

"Annabelle!"

Annabelle started, her wide-eyed gaze riveted on Samuel's face. "I've got to go."

Chapter 13

Annabelle stared at the telegram from Lucy's father, telling them not to come to Illinois. A blizzard had shut down all train travel into Chicago.

"Well, if that don't just beat all," Aunt Eugenia sputtered. "Jack, you might as well turn this wagon around and take us home."

"Yes ma'am."

Jack was uncharacteristically quiet, but what could he say? No amount of teasing or joking would change things.

Aunt Eugenia patted Annabelle's gloved hand. "What a pity, Annabelle. I know how much you had your heart set on spending time with Lucy. But you'll get another chance. Maybe this summer would be a good time to visit, much better than the dead of winter."

Annabelle nodded, not trusting herself to speak. When would she get another chance? School was due to start back in two weeks and would run all the way into May. And Aunt Eugenia didn't realize that it was a white Christmas she longed for just as much as she longed to see her cousin.

How ironic.

The very thing she longed for—snow—was the very thing that was keeping her from her dream. And Christmas only came once a year. What would next year bring? Where would she be by then? What if she never got another chance at a white Christmas?

I will be content, Lord.

She searched her heart for the bitter disappointment that she expected to feel and was surprised to discover her regret wasn't as keen as it would have been a week ago. All the way to town, she'd listened to Aunt Eugenia's prattle, answered her aunt's questions. But in the lulls, when Aunt Eugenia got wound up on one tale or another that Annabelle could recite in her sleep, her mind wandered.

Straight back to Samuel and the kiss they'd shared.

Samuel.

Like a two-by-four fresh off the saw blade, his kiss had knocked her upside the heart and made her realize what a dolt she'd been. She'd been so caught up in her own girlish dreams and plans that she'd failed to pay attention to what was right in front of her.

Well, that wasn't quite true. She *had* noticed how

he'd teased her and held her close when she'd almost fallen, but she'd decided that her own romantic notions of wanting a beau had clouded her vision and that Samuel didn't feel anything more for her than a brotherly-type love because he was Jack's partner.

Her cheeks flamed. His kiss had been anything but brotherly.

"Annabelle, are you listening?"

She started, realizing they'd pulled up in front of her aunt's house. "I'm sorry, Aunt Eugenia, my mind wandered."

Her aunt gave her an understanding smile. "You're forgiven. I was saying that you and Jack are welcome to spend the night with me. It'll be dark by the time you get home."

Annabelle shook her head. She just wanted to be home in her own bed to nurse her disappointment. "Thank you—"

"We'd better head on home, Aunt Eugenia." Jack jumped down from the wagon and helped their aunt down, then reached into the wagon for her bags. "Samuel and I need to be in the woods by daylight."

"Of course, I wasn't thinking. You've already lost a day of work, Jack, and Annabelle and I appreciate it."

They said their good-byes, and Jack urged the horses

toward home. They rode in silence for a while, before he slanted a look her way. "You're mighty quiet."

Annabelle shrugged. "Disappointed, that's all."

"Ah, sis, I know how much this trip meant to you." Jack jostled her shoulder. "Sorry it didn't work out like you planned."

She threw him a surprised look. "Thanks, Jack."

He tossed her a teasing grin. "See, I can be just as sweet as Samuel when I want to be."

Annabelle laughed along with him, grateful for the gathering twilight that masked the blistering heat that swooshed up her neck and flooded her cheekbones. "The key is that you rarely want to be."

The miles passed quickly, the jingle of the harness and the *clop-clop* of the horses' hooves filling the silence as they topped the ridge a mile north of the sawmill. Would Samuel still be there? Would Jack stop? Her heart pounded. How could she face Samuel this soon after he'd kissed her?

She clasped her hands tightly in her lap and prayed Jack wouldn't stop. They continued on, the wagon creaking as dusk fell quickly. Her heart pounded as the squat barn-like structure came into view, dark, no smoke rising from the smokestack. Samuel had closed up shop for the night and gone home. As they plodded on past, Annabelle closed her eyes in relief. She needed time to think before she saw him again.

Because above and beyond thoughts of the kiss they'd shared, and the way his touch sent her heart rate spiraling out of control, one panicky thought rose to the surface. Why hadn't he said anything? If he cared for her, why hadn't he declared himself instead of letting her go? Her cheeks heated as the thought flitted through her brain.

Maybe he had declared himself, not with words, but with actions.

Chapter 14

Come daylight, Samuel and Jack were in the woods harvesting their first tree of the day. Jack whistled a merry tune, and Samuel poured his frustration into pushing the crosscut saw toward his partner, then pulling it back with just as much gusto.

Jack had plenty to be happy about. But with Annabelle gone, Samuel didn't expect to enjoy Christmas very much. And he'd made things worse by kissing her yesterday. He clenched his jaw as he jerked the saw toward himself. Not that he regretted kissing her—not by a long shot—but now he had two full weeks to stew on how she felt about it, and what he'd do about it when she returned.

He scowled at Jack. "What are you so happy about?"

Jack grinned. "I'm going to ask Maggie to marry me on Christmas Eve. I don't have a ring yet, but she won't mind when she finds out that we're building her a house."

"We?"

"Of course." Jack pushed the saw toward Samuel. "I'll return the favor when it's your turn. Which reminds me. You haven't asked about Annabelle this morning."

Samuel thrust the blade back and sawdust flew, the rhythmic, rasping sound filling the forest. "There's really nothing to ask. I'm sure you got her and her aunt on the train without incident. They're probably in Illinois by now."

"Nope."

Samuel's gaze sharpened. "What's that supposed to mean?"

"They didn't go. Blizzard in Illinois halted all train travel." Jack gave the saw a shove toward Samuel. "So, maybe now you can see about courting my sister like you should have done already."

Annabelle hadn't gone to Illinois.

She was still here, in Mississippi, at home, less than two miles away as the crow flies. His heart pounded, and it wasn't from the push-pull exertion of working the saw. He wanted to ask Jack if she'd been disappointed, but he already knew the answer to that question. Of course she was. A white Christmas was all she'd talked about for weeks, for months.

And he'd kissed her.

Then thought he had two weeks for the image to fade.

What was he going to do now?

Chapter 15

Annabelle unpacked her carpetbags, folded her clothes, and put them away. She fingered the thick twine tied around Samuel's present. Should she take it back and tell him to just give it to her on Christmas morning?

Taking the present back would be silly, and how would she face him, alone, at the sawmill? Or worse, in front of Jack?

No, she'd wait until Christmas Day. Since his mother had moved to the other side of Newton to live with her sister, he'd probably spend Christmas with her family anyway, just as he had for the last two years. At least on Christmas morning, her family would be around, and she wouldn't feel quite so awkward when she opened it. And, maybe, just maybe, the two of them could move forward after that. If. . .if that was what he wanted.

"Annabelle?" her mother called from the kitchen.

"Yes ma'am? Coming." She left the package on top of her hope chest and headed down the hall.

"Lilly's awake." Her mother, hands busy kneading a lump of dough, nodded at Annabelle's little sister. The toddler's grasping hands pulled at her mother's skirt. Lilly spotted Annabelle, let go of her mother, and toddled toward her sister.

Annabelle picked her up and hugged her. "Hello, sunshine."

"Run and gather the eggs, would you?" Her mother deftly flipped the dough over and continued working it with her fingers. "As soon as I set this bread to rising, I want to get some baking done. Christmas will be here before you know it."

Annabelle lowered Lilly to her pallet and handed her a pan and a wooden spoon.

Her mother cringed at the first bang. "Oh, goodness, Annabelle, not that."

"Sorry, Mama, it's the only thing that keeps her busy and out of trouble." She laughed as she grabbed a coat off a peg by the door.

"And Annabelle?"

"Yes ma'am?"

"I know you're disappointed that your trip didn't work out, but I'm glad you'll be home for Christmas. I wasn't looking forward to having you gone, you know."

"Thanks, Mama."

They shared a smile before Annabelle hurried to the chicken coop to gather the eggs. It didn't take long, and she re-entered the kitchen, eggs in hand. Her mother peered into the basket and counted. "Hmm, I was hoping for more. We'll all have to make do with one fried egg each the next few days if I'm going to get my baking done."

"For your Christmas cookies and pound cake, I'll do without an egg all week."

Her mother laughed. "I don't think it'll come to that."

Annabelle took off her coat and put the eggs away. Lilly sat in the corner on her pallet, banging her spoon against the pot and squealing with delight. Annabelle smiled as she tied an apron around her waist. "Where is everybody?"

"They went to the gristmill." Her mother put the dough in a pan, covered it with a piece of cheesecloth, and set it to the side. "I was glad to see them go. With school out, they've been like a pack of wild coyotes. I told Hiram that when they get back, I want him to put the boys to work cleaning out the barn."

Before long, the kitchen smelled of baking bread, sugar cookies, and the pot of vegetable soup simmering on the stove for the noon meal. Annabelle went to the well and brought in a fresh pail of water, relieved that Lilly had stopped her banging.

She washed her hands, reached for a kitchen towel, and removed a sheet of cookies from the oven. The fresh-baked aroma of butter mingled with sugar made her mouth water. "Maybe we'll get all these cookies out of sight before Papa and the boys get back. Otherwise, there won't be any left for Christmas."

"Why do you think I sent them all to town this morning?" Her mother laughed as she rolled more dough, her hands covered in flour. She jerked her head toward the hall. "Check on Lilly, if you don't mind. She slipped out a few minutes ago while you were outside."

"Lilly?" Annabelle stepped into the hallway, calling for her baby sister. The family room was empty and the door to the small room where her father prayed and planned his sermons was shut. Her heart lurched as her gaze jerked to the stairs that led to the attic rooms the boys slept in. Had Lilly managed to climb the stairs?

"Lilly? Where are you, sweetie?"

The door to the room she shared with Sally was ajar, and relief filled her when she heard a rustling inside. She found her little sister seated in the middle of the room, Samuel's present clasped in her chubby little hands.

Lilly grinned at Annabelle, patting the present. "Mine."

"No, Lilly." Annabelle laughed, plucked her sister up, and examined the torn paper.

"Mine," Lilly repeated.

"No, you little scamp. It's not yours."

Lilly giggled again and lunged for the present, her grasping hands tearing the wrapping paper even more before Annabelle could get it way from her. She propped her sister on her hip and cradled the package in the other hand, the half-torn paper revealing the top of a canning jar. She frowned.

A canning jar?

Samuel had given her a canning jar for Christmas?

Unable to contain her curiosity, she pulled back the paper to peek at the contents. She gasped, letting Lilly slide to the floor. Lilly happily plopped down and played with the discarded paper. Annabelle held the jar, mesmerized by the miniature scene inside.

A tiny carved church, complete with steeple, lay submerged in water, a winding trail leading down and around as if following the curve of a hill. She turned the jar to see the next scene. Her heart lurched as she spotted what looked like the sawmill, with a lean-to tacked on the side. Miniature carved trees, painted green, pointed straight and tall toward the sky, looking lifelike behind and around the buildings. Another rotation and the schoolhouse came into view, nestled among a stand of evergreens.

She held the jar up to the light streaming in the bedroom window. Sawdust shavings covered the base of the carving like a dusting of snow. Annabelle's breath caught as she saw the tiny flakes swirling in the water as if kicked up by a gentle wind.

Mesmerized, she gently turned the jar upside down, and the sawdust floated to the top of the water. When she turned it right side up, the tiny flakes fell slowly, landing softly on the trees, the church, the sawmill, coating the entire scene just like a cascade of falling snow.

She blinked back tears as she cradled the jar in both hands. Samuel had given her a white Christmas, right here in the evergreen forest in the heart of Mississippi.

Chapter 16

The door to the sawmill creaked open and Samuel turned from putting the finishing touches on Mrs. Denson's rocking chair. "Forget something?"

But it wasn't Jack who stood in the doorway. Annabelle stood there, the sun that had just dipped below the tips of the evergreen trees casting a red and gold aura around her. She moved toward him, the canning jar in her hands, and he could only stand still and wait.

She moved closer, away from the sun that blocked her face from his view, and he saw the smile on her lips and the way her green eyes shone with joy.

A physical ache tugged at him when she looked away, held the canning jar aloft, flipped it, then righted it, letting the sawdust flutter in the small container. Her smile widened and he swallowed, remembering how soft her lips had felt when he'd kissed her, wondering how she felt about that kiss now. Surely if she hated him for it, she wouldn't have come, would she?

Her gaze left the tiny scene in the jar and captured

his. "You made this for me? Why?"

Why?

To bring you back to me.

He settled for something less risky. "To give you something to remember home by."

"It's lovely." She cradled the jar and smiled at him. "Thank you."

"You're welcome."

"And, just so you know, I didn't open it early. Lilly found it in my room." Her look was apologetic. "I hope you're not disappointed."

"I could never be disappointed in you, Annabelle."

She dipped her head and asked shyly, "Why didn't you say something?"

Samuel's heart pounded. "About what?"

"About us. About my trip." Her face flamed, and she ran a finger along the back of a chair. "Even when— when . . . you kissed me, you didn't say anything."

"Ah, Annabelle, you'd had your heart set on that trip to Illinois for so long. That's all you've ever wanted, was to have a white Christmas."

"So, you wanted me to go?"

"Well, not exactly." He choked back a laugh. "But it was what you wanted."

"What if it's not what I want anymore?"

His heart thudded against his ribcage as her eyes met and held his. He closed the distance between them, his gaze flickering to her lips, and back again. He cupped her face with the palm of his hand. "What do you want, Annabelle?"

She reached out a hand and rested it against his shirtfront, and he thought his heart would pound right out of his chest.

"I don't know what I want, but maybe"—tears shimmered in her beautiful green eyes, but she held his gaze, searching, looking—"maybe between the two of us we can figure it out."

Samuel lowered his lips to hers and did a bit of figuring of his own.

Epilogue

One Year Later

The whistle blew as the train passed through another small, sleepy town on its journey north. Annabelle smiled at Samuel, slumbering beside her. The train rocked on through the night, a hint of dawn peeping through the drawn curtains. Come daylight, they'd be in Illinois, spending their first Christmas as a married couple with Lucy and her family.

Samuel stirred, and her heart fluttered. She smoothed back his dark hair, desperately in need of a trim, and then ran one finger down his cheek, rough with day-old stubble. Not much opportunity to shave on the train. But she liked the hint of whiskers on his face. His lips quirked, and she jerked her gaze upward and found him watching her through heavy-lidded eyes.

"Morning, Mrs. Frazier."

Her stomach dipped at the gravelly sound of his voice, roughened by sleep. "Mr. Frazier."

"Happy?" He wrapped his arms around her, and she laid her head on his rumpled shirt.

"Very." Annabelle smiled. She was more than happy. She was content. Very, very content.

They lay still, the rocking motion of the train lulling Annabelle back into half-wakeful, half-asleep slumber. The past year had been like a dream. Samuel had courted her in his quiet, determined way all through spring while helping Jack build a house. Jack and Maggie had married as soon as their house was finished, a stone's throw from the sawmill.

Come June, Annabelle had walked down the aisle and become Samuel's bride, and they'd moved into their own home built from lumber cut from the mill. Money was tight, but the business was flourishing, and they were blissfully happy. And then Samuel had announced they were going to Illinois for Christmas.

Annabelle smiled, listening to the steady thrum of her husband's heartbeat. Yes, she was excited about the trip, and yes, she wanted to see her cousin, but she didn't need a white Christmas anymore.

She'd always be Samuel's evergreen bride, her hopes and dreams forever planted in the pine forest way down in the heart of Mississippi.

About the Author

Pam Hillman was born and raised on a dairy farm in Mississippi and spent her teenage years perched on the seat of a tractor, raking hay. In those days, her daddy couldn't afford two cab tractors with air conditioning and a radio, so Pam drove an old Allis Chalmers 110. When her daddy asked her if she wanted to bale hay, she told him she didn't mind raking. Raking hay doesn't take much thought, so Pam spent her time working on her tan and making up stories in her head. Please visit Pam at www.pamhillman.com

The Yuletide Bride

By Michelle Ule

For Rachel Durham,
And the fine musicians of St. Mark Lutheran Church
Including
Lynn, David, Marianne, Lou, Helen,
and
the Jubilate choir

Chapter 1

Fairhope, Nebraska 1873

Ewan Murray's fingers shook so much, he had trouble tightening the tuning nut on his fiddle. After four long months, the moment he'd dreamed of beckoned. Surely she wouldn't be late to church.

He plucked the strings, winced at one out of tune, adjusted the instrument, and picked up the horsehair bow. When the front door open, a breeze blew in the scent of ripening corn, and Ewan's heart began to hammer.

"As soon as the MacDougalls are seated, you can start," Reverend Cummings said. "We're pleased to have you and your violin back."

Ewan nodded but he scarcely took in the words, so transfixed was he by the refined young woman coming down the aisle behind her burly father. With her auburn hair swept into a knot, his childhood playmate, Kate MacDougall, had grown into a woman.

Her eyes widened. He laughed to watch her bite

back a delighted squeal. She'd seen him, too.

With bow poised over the strings, he waited as Kate, her older brother, Malcom, and their parents filed into a second-row pew. Kate smoothed her blue silk skirt and lifted her face—and heart, he was sure of it—to him as he slid through the opening notes of "Amazing Grace."

Had he ever played with such emotion? Ewan's heart soared with joy and hope, God's grace bestowed upon the hundred church members, and for Kate.

He played only for her.

And God, of course!

Reverend Cummings raised an eyebrow at Ewan's breathless finish. Ewan took a seat in the first pew, acutely aware of Kate directly behind him. He struggled to concentrate, but eventually God's Word focused his thoughts and he spoke the Lord's Prayer with enthusiasm. The sermon, as always, engaged his mind and left him excited at what God had ordained for him.

And for Kate, too. He tossed a sly look over his shoulder.

She dimpled. He caught a whiff of lilac.

Duncan MacDougall cleared his throat. Ewan faced forward.

During the passing of the plate, Ewan played "Blest

Be the Tie That Binds," lingering perhaps too long on the vibrato, but happiness swelled and he could scarce contain himself.

Until he looked across the aisle at Josiah Finch and his fingers faltered. Why was the son of the wealthiest man in the county casting eyes at his Kate?

He swayed to look in her direction. She batted her thick eyelashes and blushed.

So there, Josiah.

Reverend Cummings spoke the benediction and Ewan launched into "Jesus, Lover of My Soul," to end the service. Perhaps he sped through it, but he needed to speak to Kate.

And also to Duncan MacDougall. Ewan gulped and thought of his mother's prayer: "I put this situation in your hands, Lord, come what may."

As the congregation filed out, Ewan rubbed down his instrument with his mother's old embroidered handkerchief and nestled both into the battered case.

"Will you play next week? Perhaps you and young Kate could perform a duet? We've missed your fine music this summer."

Ewan tugged on his coat, the last garment his mother had sewn, now a little tight with his nine-teenth birthday. "I'll speak to Kate. It's sheer joy to play with her."

"You wear your heart on your sleeve, Ewan. Be careful."

He tucked the case under his arm and thanked the minister who had been so kind through the last difficult years. Reverend Cummings had buried his parents and given him a bed in his barn. He knew Ewan's circumstances and Ewan trusted him.

Ewan put on his old summer hat and stepped onto the wide church porch to survey the area. Golden fields surrounded the churchyard, while on the wide lawn facing town ladies spread a potluck luncheon across makeshift tables. Ewan ignored his grumbling stomach to search for his prize.

She'd put up a parasol while politely listening to Josiah Finch, but her attention flitted his way. Her proud mercantile owner father stood behind, his satisfied hands tucked into his linen vest and a straw hat pushed back from his forehead.

"Ewan, it's good to see you again." Mrs. MacDougall carried a basket of heavenly scented biscuits. "Have you returned for good?"

"I hope so, ma'am." He took the basket and set it on the closest table. "Kate looks beautiful."

"She does." Mrs. MacDougall's voice lowered.

"Josiah Fitch who works for the bank in Clarkesville, has come calling. Duncan is pleased."

His stomach roiled. Ewan cleared his throat. "How does Kate feel about him?"

"It would be a good match."

Ewan's heart sank. She'd always been kind.

"But who can know a young woman's heart?" Mrs. MacDougall's dimple matched her daughter's as she glided away.

"Ewan!" Kate danced across the grass to grasp his free hand. "You've been gone so long. I've missed you. I've had no one to make music with."

An auburn curl had escaped her hairpins and dangled above her rounded shoulder. He tucked it behind her ear, nearly catching the lock on her sparkling ear bob. "We'll have to remedy that." His voice sounded hoarse.

She leaned forward. "Are you back for good?"

"I hope so. Are you glad to see me?"

Kate glanced toward her father. "Absolutely. I've made three sweet new flutes. Call after the social and bring your fiddle; so much has changed this summer."

"I can see." His heart hammered and tongue twisted. It was safer to stay with simple answers.

She bit her full, pink lips. "Will you sit with me

at supper? Josiah will probably join us, but you won't mind, will you?"

He could see Finch glowering at him. "I must speak with your father, first."

"Hurry. He's always hungry after the service."

Ewan took a deep breath and approached the Fairhope founder.

"You played well," MacDougall said. "Your parents would have been pleased."

"Thank you, sir. May I have a word with you in private?"

"Now?"

"If possible."

MacDougall indicated the plain wooden church topped with a bell. "We can speak on the other side of the building."

As far as the eye could see, a healthy crop of corn stretched golden and ripe under the clear blue sky. As the son of a farmer, Ewan knew the harvest would begin soon. "A good crop."

"A fine one. I assume you've come to work."

"Yes, sir."

"I'm sure we can find you a spot."

"Thank you, sir, and I'll take you up on that, but . . ." Ewan took a deep breath and tried to calm the nervous butterflies Mr. MacDougall always provoked. "I'd like to talk about Kate."

The older man beamed. "My girl is growing up. She's doing a fine job at the mercantile. Our little schoolhouse taught you well." MacDougall frowned. "Other than Malcolm, of course. But he'll come into his own when he runs the mercantile."

Ewan raised his eyebrows. "Malcolm will run the store?"

MacDougall scratched the back of his neck. "He just needs time to grow up. He'll drive a wagonload of goods to Sterling tomorrow. You remember how he loves horses."

"Yes."

"He could use a teamster. Perhaps you'd like to help him? It'll be overnight, but I'll pay you five dollars."

"I'd like the work."

"Good. Let's eat."

"I have another question."

MacDougall tapped his toes.

"I'd like to ask for Kate's hand."

The large man stared. "My Kate?"

Ewan removed his old hat and brushed the unruly dark curls off his brow. "I've loved her since I was a boy. I'm a man now and would like to wed her."

"Ewan, you've had a rough go of it, but you're just a grasshopper of a boy. You've no land, no prospects, no money. All you've got is your fiddle and a willing heart. It's not enough to court my daughter."

"We love each other, sir. You know we do. We've always planned to wed."

"Childhood fantasies, Ewan. Surely you can see how ridiculous this suggestion is? Josiah Fitch is a much better prospect. How would you support my daughter?"

"I'll do anything. I'm a hard worker."

MacDougall frowned and stared at the ground. "I can't do it, Ewan. You can't live on love. Unless you can support my girl, I'd be a poor father to agree."

Ewan clenched and unclenched his hands, but kept his voice steady. "What would it take, sir? How can I prove myself?"

Behind them, the scratchy sound of insects in the corn caught Ewan's ear. A soaring red hawk called from above and came to rest on the top of the church. Enormous piles of white clouds built across the horizon. Ewan waited, praying for God to give him the desire of his heart.

MacDougall sighed in a great gust. "I mark your words, Ewan. I knew your family, good people. I've always been sorry for your loss. But unless you can earn seventy dollars by Kate's Christmas birthday, I cannot agree to a match."

"Seventy dollars?" Ewan had never earned so much in all his fiddling days. He barely had fifteen dollars to his name and it needed to last the winter. To suggest a lesser amount, however, would insult Kate and worsen his chances. He swallowed across an enormous lump in his throat. "It's a deal. Seventy dollars and Kate will be my Yuletide bride."

The older man winced. "I'm sorry it has to be this way."

Ewan put out his hand. MacDougall shook it.

"Know this, Ewan," MacDougall said as they walked to the tables. "Josiah Finch has already asked."

Chapter 2

Kate tried to be patient, she really did, but she hadn't spent any time with Ewan since he'd finished the June planting and left to find work. She could hardly wait to play her flute and accompany him on his fiddle. It had been hard to sit still in church, she so itched to join him. Perhaps Reverend Cummings would let her sing next week with Ewan. Without Ewan's music, the long summer had been empty and quiet.

She paced along the edge of the grass, watching Ewan and her father. What could they be discussing to take so long? Josiah could swoop in and spirit her away if Ewan didn't hurry.

"Malcolm," she whispered. Her brawny older brother always smelled of his prized horses. "Go distract Josiah."

He grimaced. "What can I talk to him about?"

"Tell him about your team."

"He doesn't want to talk to your brother, but I'll try."

Kate closed her parasol and thrust it at him. "Take

this with you and tell him it needs to be tweaked. He loves to pretend he can fix things."

With a grunt, Malcolm strolled to the well-dressed young man loitering at the lemonade table. Josiah eagerly snatched the parasol to examine it while her brother stood motionless and awkward, hands in his pockets. Kate glanced back to the church where Ewan and her father shook hands.

Kate took a deep breath and felt the pinch of the new stays. Her blue silk dress belled out in the breeze and the scent of ripening corn filled the air. The busiest time of year was coming. Would Ewan have time to play?

Ewan carried his battered fiddle case and rubbed his chin with his right index finger as he walked across the grass. Ewan's hands were always in motion, practically a blur when he played a fast tune.

He set down the case, propped his hat on top, and took her hands. She rubbed his finger calluses even as she felt an unexpected jolt at his touch. "Why so sober? Can my father not help you?"

"In this one, no." His sky blue eyes looked troubled, his black brows tense. Ewan's shoulders had broadened during the summer though he still stood only several inches taller than Kate. His confident merriment usually buoyed her, but today he seemed tentative.

"What is it? Do you need a place to stay?"

He shook his head. "Reverend Cummings has given me the extra room in his barn. It's a good place for now. But not for the future." Ewan wrinkled his tanned forehead.

"Mama's made fried chicken and her feather-light biscuits. I churned the sweet butter myself. Let's fill our plates and you can tell me about your summer. Where have you been?"

"I must speak with you alone."

She dimpled. "Here I am. Speak away."

Ewan swallowed and lowered his rich tenor voice. "Haven't we always made beautiful music together?"

"Yes." Mirth bubbled.

"Would you like to do it forever? With me?"

"Of course."

His mouth dropped open. "Then you'll do it? Just like that?"

"Play music with you? Of course. I've missed you so much. I made three new reed flutes this summer, but it wasn't the same without you here."

Ewan squeezed her hands. "No. I mean, yes. But, that's not what I'm asking."

She scrutinized him. His thick black hair was rough

with curls, but he gazed with such intensity and, could it be, longing? Josiah stared at her the same way, as if he would swallow her whole. She always slipped away from him, uncomfortable. But this was Ewan with whom she'd laughed, sang, and fluted so many happy days.

She caught her breath at a new thought.

Ewan took a matching breath.

Kate gripped his hands as the idea surged through to her soul. "Are you asking me to wed you?"

His hands shook and he nodded.

She leaned toward him. "Were you discussing marriage with Papa?"

He nodded again. She'd never known Ewan to lose his tongue.

Excitement poured through Kate. If she married Ewan, dear, darling Ewan, they could have a home of their own filled with music. Ewan could fiddle every night and she would accompany him. Music would surround her all day long. The children they could produce, musicians all!

"Oh, Ewan," she sighed. "Most definitely, yes."

"It's time for the potluck, Kate." Josiah's deep voice, a bass, broke into their conversation. "I'll escort you."

Dazed, she faced him. "What?"

"Sunday dinner." Josiah pressed his lips together in disapproval. "You played well today, Ewan."

"Thank you. Kate is dining with me."

"With me."

Kate cut them off. "With both of you. Shall we get our plates?"

Her heart beat so fast, Kate thought she would faint. She led the two men—suitors, she realized—to the potluck line. Her father waited with arms crossed.

"Papa, do you know?"

"We'll discuss this later. Reverend Cummings is about to pray."

As it did no good to antagonize Josiah or his family, Kate followed him to a seat with Ewan right behind. "We need three seats together, Josiah."

Josiah waved his free hand. "Ewan can sit any-where."

"I'll bring a chair from another table." Ewan set down his plate and retrieved it.

Josiah scowled until he realized how close Kate needed to sit to him.

As she nestled between the two handsome men, her toes danced in her slippers. She yearned to hear Ewan's stories, listen to his fiddle, and dream about the future. Stories about the summer would do for now.

She'd spent so much time listening to Josiah talk about his activities, he could listen to Ewan's adventures with her. "Tell me where you've been," Kate asked at the same moment Josiah demanded, "Why did you come back?"

Ewan's eyes twinkled at Kate. "I've played for summer dances and church festivals in four counties. One of the camp meetings featured a choir of plump women who loved the fiddle. They sounded splendid and full voiced on 'My Faith Looks Up to Thee.' I kept looking to the sky myself, thinking Jesus must have been smiling down."

Josiah tried again. "What will you do in Fairhope?"

"I'm looking for work. Do you have a job I could do?"

"What can a fiddler do other than play his toy?"

Ewan stuck out his chin. "I have a teaching certificate. I'm good at ciphering. I can work in a store, help with the harvest. Tomorrow I'm teaming with Malcolm to haul a wagonload of goods to Sterling."

"You are?" Kate squeaked. "Malcolm will be so pleased."

Josiah relaxed. "Is that what you were discussing with Mr. MacDougall?"

"Yes."

The stilted conversation continued. Josiah expounded on issues at the small bank where he worked in Clarkesville, the county seat, and his travels around the county "drumming up" business.

"So you don't live in Fairhope?" Ewan asked.

"I ride the train home on weekends to worship in this fine church," he paused. "And to see Kate, of course."

She blushed. He'd begun paying attention to her only since her schooling ended in June, and had shown a marked interest when she put up her hair.

"I think you'd enjoy living in Clarkesville, Kate."

Kate frowned. She hated it when Josiah acted pompous. "I've never given Clarkesville any thought. I love Fairhope. I know my neighbors here."

"But you're so friendly and welcoming. I'm sure you'd be popular wherever you lived."

Kate didn't know how to answer. She touched Ewan's arm and stood. "Could we sing? Get your fiddle and we'll start a sing-along."

Ewan retrieved his instrument. He rosined the bow and quietly began a favorite: "In the Sweet By and By."

"There's a land that is fairer than day," Kate sang.

The folks still sitting under the trees sang in four-part harmony. Ewan's fiddle led the melody, and they sang for half an hour.

Kate swayed with the tunes. When she met Ewan's gaze, happiness coursed through her. Surely, helping Ewan lead worship is what God had created her to do.

They packed up the baskets and their possessions as the afternoon grew late. First Josiah and then Ewan pressed her hand, promising to call later. Kate sighed as her family carried baskets full of leftovers, plates, cups, and cutlery down the wide dirt road to their home behind the mercantile.

"Ewan said he spoke with you, Papa. I'm so happy."

"What did he say?" Mama asked.

Papa shifted the basket from one hand to the other. "He'll ride teamster with Malcolm tomorrow. I'm paying him five dollars for the trip."

"Great." Malcolm said.

Kate set her jaw. "He asked for my hand, Papa. I told him yes."

Mama gasped.

Kate turned on her. "You know I've always cared for Ewan."

She nodded.

Papa's brows drew together. "There's a catch, Kate. He cannot marry you unless he's earned seventy dollars by your eighteenth birthday."

Kate went still. So much money! No wonder he'd seemed worried. She drew herself up tall. "I have confidence in my Ewan. He'll earn the money and I'll be a Christmas bride. I know it."

Papa raised his eyebrows. "We'll find out, won't we?"

Chapter 3

Ewan met Malcolm behind the MacDougall Mercantile early the next morning. They filled his wagon with a pickle barrel, crates of dry goods, bags of flour, and other staples. Malcolm retrieved his well-brushed horses, harnessed them to the wagon, and they set off on the long dusty road to Sterling.

Already, farmers worked their fields, preparing for the harvest. A torrent of jackrabbits scattered as they passed. Calling birds sailed on the wing as the sun rose slowly in the eastern sky. Ewan savored the cool, fresh scent of a September morning.

"You still got your mare?" Malcolm asked.

"Yep. Tess is cropping grass in the Reverend's back forty today. We traveled a far distance this summer."

"I remember when your pa got that horse. I never saw one so beautiful in my life. You let me know if you ever want to sell her."

His throat thickened when he thought of his parents now two years gone. "She's a beauty all right."

Malcolm nodded. "I'd rather spend all day with a

horse than sit in the mercantile. If my pa has his way, I'll go crazy."

Ewan watched his old friend chew on a piece of fresh straw. "What's the problem?"

"I never did learn how to cipher. The numbers swim in front of me and I get lost. Horses are better. They don't care if you can add or subtract."

"Adding and subtracting is the problem?"

He shrugged. "I can do it if I think long enough. But I don't well remember how to multiply and divide. You remember how Mr. Bellows used to hit me with a cane?"

"Yes." Ewan often felt the slash of the same cane for not sitting still in class. "What if I helped you?"

Malcolm sighed. "No one can help me. I'm stupid."

"Once you understand the concept and memorize the multiplication tables, it starts to make sense. The trick is to get into the rhythm. Try it. One times one is. . ."

He waited.

Malcolm shrugged.

"One," Ewan said. "One times two is?"

"Two?"

"Exactly." Ewan sang through the times tables in time to the harness jingle. "Two times two is four; two times three is six; two times four is eight."

They worked on memorizing the multiplication tables through twelve. Ewan beat on the wagon, sang to the rhythm, called out the numbers and encouraged his friend. The *clip-clop* of the horses' hooves provided a steady beat.

"It can't be that simple," Malcolm said.

"I'll work with you. You're intelligent. We can do this together."

Halfway to Sterling they stopped to water the horses. Ewan collected pebbles. While they ate their dinner, he demonstrated multiplication with piles of small stones. "Two times three is taking two piles of three stones and putting them together. How many do you have?"

Malcolm ran his tongue around the inside of his mouth, pondering. "Six?"

"Perfect."

While Ewan bit into his slab of spiced beef and thick, chewy bread, Malcolm arranged the stones into three piles of four each. "Twelve?"

Ewan nodded. "Try five times six."

The young man's brow furrowed as he moved the stones around. Ewan shook his head. Twenty years old and no one had ever explained how arithmetic worked.

When Malcolm shouted and grinned, Ewan knew he had grasped the concept—probably for the first time.

"Five times five is twenty-five; five times six is thirty. I just have to memorize the answers and I know?" The wonder in Malcolm's voice troubled Ewan.

"Exactly. We'll practice all the way to Sterling. I bet you'll have it down by the time we get there."

He did.

"How come no one ever explained it like this before?" Malcolm asked as they put up the sweaty horses that night at a livery stable.

Ewan shrugged. "You keep singing the song and memorizing the numbers. The next time we team together, we'll work on division."

"Wouldn't that be something?" Malcom said. "But I still don't want to leave the horses. I love them."

Ewan felt the same way about his fiddle.

∞

"I know Ewan can earn the money," Kate said. "He's always been clever and resourceful."

"Seventy dollars is a large sum," Mama said. "How much does he earn fiddling?"

Kate didn't know, and she'd hardly had time to talk to Ewan alone since his stuttered proposal on Sunday. "He can work the harvest and find other odd jobs.

People always need help."

They sat together quietly while Kate chewed on her lip and tried to think what Ewan could do.

Fairhope was a small town. The mercantile was the biggest enterprise and most folks lived on farms. Ewan couldn't be the minister. He had received a primary teaching certificate last fall, but dedicated spinster Doris Hall schoolmarmed the grammar school east of town near the bend in the stream. Mr. Storner taught the secondary school in town.

"Maybe he could work at the train station?"

Her mother frowned. "Those jobs are taken."

"I'll give him my job," Kate declared.

"Your father wouldn't agree," Mama said. "You know he wants Ewan to demonstrate he can provide for you without our help."

Kate threw herself onto the soft velvet settee. "What am I going to do? How can I help him? Don't you think he's the perfect man for me?"

Mama sat beside her. "I loved his mother as my dearest friend. I know he's a fine young man. If you're adult enough to wed, Kate, you need to think about what it means to be a helpmeet."

She pondered the word *helpmeet*. Obviously the Bible passage meant a wife should assist her husband.

How could she help him? What could she do to encourage Ewan to work hard for them both?

Kate savored the thrilling thought he was working for her. It was like Jacob in the Bible. Except, he wound up with two brides. Kate chuckled. That wouldn't happen. Ewan only looked at Kate; he never even saw other girls.

"Could I make my wedding dress? It would cheer him if he knew I expected to wear the dress at Christmas time."

"What a lovely gesture," Mama said. "There's fabric in your grandmother's old trunk. Let's see if it's suitable."

Kate pulled the trunk from the dark corner of the attic and set it on the floor of her bedroom.

"After your grandmother died, your father couldn't bear to remember his heritage. It made him feel too sad."

"Will Papa mind?"

"No. He's always meant you to have *Guiddame's* prize possessions."

Kate lifted the lid. Her father's mother loved the dried lavender tucked inside.

"Such fine cloth." Mama unfolded the red and green plaid with lines of royal blue. "Perfect for Christmas."

Kate lifted the soft wool to her shoulders. "There's plenty for a dress."

"Your Guiddame would be pleased you like it."

"What have we here?" Papa stood in the doorway.

"Kate needs a new dress for winter, and I remembered this fabric."

"The MacDougall tartan," he said. "I once had a cap made of the plaid."

"Do you mind, Papa?"

He shook his head. "Let's see what else is in the trunk." He pulled out an old leather volume. "The family Bible." Turning the musty pages, he paused at the names written in dark ink. "Her death was the last item on the list. Your birth the one before." He turned the book for Kate to see.

"Why is it in the attic instead of in the parlor where we can read it?"

He shrugged. "It should come out. Enough time has gone by I don't miss her with such a sharp ache. She'd be on me for hiding away this Bible."

Kate knelt beside her mother and reached into the chest for a large deerskin bag. "What's this?"

She struggled to contain the bundle of old leather and wooden sticks as she lifted it out. She turned to her father, who barked a bitter laugh. "I'd think you, of all people, would recognize a musical instrument. Bagpipes."

She peered closer and saw round holes in one of the sticks. Turning the bundle over, four wooden tubes jutted out the back of what appeared to be a flattened sack covered in the MacDougall plaid. One stick had small holes on the capped end and the other three tubes had knobby endings.

"You must blow in these holes, but what is this sack the sticks are attached to?"

He pursed his lips in distaste. "Bellows. You blow into the mouthpiece, place the bag under your arm and manage the sound by squeezing out the air." He pointed to the finger holed stick. "You play the notes there on the chanter. The longer tubes on top are drones. They make low bass and tenor notes under your melody."

Papa helped her hold all the awkward pieces in place.

The short mouthpiece smelled musty and reedy, but when she blew into it, the bag expanded under her arm. She blew and blew to fill the bag until her lungs ached and she felt dizzy. A squawk sounded and Mama's hands flew to her cheeks.

Papa laughed. "After all this time, you'll need to make new reeds if you want to get any sort of melody.

I give them to you, Kate. The pipes are your heritage, but I will not listen to such caterwauling in my house. Take them away!"

Kate clasped the jumbled instrument to her chest. "Thank you."

He laughed again. "We'll see if the neighbors feel the same."

Chapter 4

Ewan winced as Kate blew into the bagpipes. The scolding, harsh sound grated on him as she wavered the tone, trying to find a clear note.

She spit out the mouthpiece in a gasp. "Don't you love it?"

"If you must make music with multiple tubes, I like the panpipes. How about a fiddle and flute duet?"

Kate set down the awkward bundle. "I'll get one."

Ewan picked up the "instrument" to examine. He observed dings and dents in the wooden tubes and was that blood on the cloth? With a little care and perhaps a new cover, it would look presentable in public, but the noise! He shuddered. His musician's ear could be both a godsend and a curse when it came to musical notes.

He tugged at the chanter and it came apart, exposing an old reed. Ewan blew, amazed it still produced a sound. He popped out the old one to study better. Surely a new reed would help the tone. In the meantime, without a reed, Kate couldn't make any noise. He grinned.

Sitting across from him, Malcolm laughed. "Thanks."

Kate sashayed into the parlor with the cane flutes she and Malcolm had constructed during the summer. Ewan knew this instrument and blew a tentative breath into the largest one. Ah, a much more satisfying sound.

The reed flutes always reminded him of his mother. She'd escort them to the creek near the school when they were children, carrying a thick knife. She'd cut the cane, whittle out holes, and they'd make music on the riverbank. Kate took to it the best, though Malcolm wasn't bad. Ewan's favorite childhood memories were of sunny days along the chattering creek piping the flutes.

"Let's play your mother's song." Kate blew the opening notes of "The Bonnie Blue Bells of Scotland." Ewan joined in, modulating his tone to ensure the notes were in tune.

Mrs. MacDougall clapped. "It reminds me of Bonnie to hear her song. You have her gift, Ewan, and it's a pleasure to hear."

"And me?" Kate asked.

"You've been well taught." Her lips lifted

in an indulgent smile.

Kate made a face and laughed with her merry mother.

Malcolm closed his eyes. "Play the number song."

Ewan tried a few notes to find the right pitch and then piped quietly while Malcolm ran through the multiplication tables.

MacDougall entered the parlor and frowned. "What's this children's song?"

"Ewan taught me to multiply."

His father challenged him on several. Malcolm got them right.

"Do you understand what it means?" MacDougall asked.

Malcolm reached for a collection of his mother's silk embroidery threads. "I'll show you. Two times two is four." He deftly moved the floss hanks into groups as he sang the multiplication tables to ten.

"So, if I have a box three feet by two feet by one foot deep, what's the volume?" His father asked.

"Take it by steps," Ewan said. "First, three times two; then the answer times one. You can figure it, Malcolm."

Mrs. MacDougall blinked rapidly.

"Three times two is six. Six times one is six.

The answer is six?"

Ewan played a piper's congratulations tune.

MacDougall stared at his son. "I don't believe it. Come to the store tomorrow and I'll put you to work."

Malcolm shook his head. "Got to get the horses shod. Sorry."

MacDougall stomped out of the room, but his wife approached Ewan. "How?"

"He needed encouragement. I don't think he'd ever grasped the concept before. He's on his way."

"But I still don't want to work in the mercantile." Malcolm rose and went upstairs.

Kate tucked her hand into Ewan's elbow as she walked him to the porch. "I'm so proud of you. Thank you for helping Malcolm."

"He'll do fine." Ewan leaned closer to her, sighing at her lilac scent, so like his mother's.

"What will you do tomorrow?"

"I'll be harvesting the Reverend's crop this week. That'll pay for my room and board," he paused, "until we're married of course. Once I'm finished there, I'll seek work at the other farms."

"I ask everyone who comes into the store if they need a worker. I'll help you."

Ewan jerked. "What type of work?"

"Anything. Right?"

He nodded. "I suppose so."

Kate inspected her slippers peeping from beneath her dark skirt. "I've found fabric to make a dress."

"You're a good seamstress."

"I know about my father's arrangement with you, and I know you can do it. I'll support you any way I can. I'm sewing a wedding dress."

Her confidence caught him by surprise. "You have such faith in me?"

She glanced toward the lighted window and dared a kiss to his cheek. "God brought us together. He'll see us to the wedding."

Ewan pressed her hand to his chest.

"Good night, Ewan," Mr. MacDougall called.

He kissed Kate's hand and jumped off the porch into a night studded with approving stars. He danced all the way to Reverend Cummings' hay-filled barn.

⋘∾⋙

Kate spent her afternoons working at her father's mercantile. She loved cutting fabric for the farm wives and watching the shy grins on children's faces when she slipped them a piece of penny candy.

When the teamster from Clarkesville stopped by with the weekly order, Kate compared the bill of lading to their ledger list. She checked off each item as she unpacked it from the crate and signed her name at the bottom. Kate swallowed when she saw the freight charges marked "C.O.D." Her father was out of the store. "How do I pay this?"

The gruff bearded man pointed to the letters. "Cash on Delivery. You pay me cash from the till, and I'll write you a receipt."

She opened the lock box, counted out the bills, and waited for the teamster to sign. He tipped his hat and left the store.

Kate tapped her fingers on the receipt. Something wasn't right.

The bell above the door rang, and a sweaty Ewan entered. "Hello, pretty girl, have you got a drink for a thirsty man?"

He smelled of summer crops and hard work; his sunburned face shone. She reached for a tin cup under the counter. "The pump is outside."

When he returned, she showed him the bill. "Does this look correct to you?"

Ewan examined the numbers. His eyebrows rose and he pointed to the freight charges. "Does it really cost this much?"

"That's what he said."

"You're paying a high percentage verses the cost of the items. It would be more economical to hire Malcolm to haul your freight."

"He'd like that," Kate said.

Ewan rubbed his chin. "This is the usual cost?"

Kate shrugged. "My father always pays this bill." She collected the papers and stuck them into the ledger. "He'll check them. I have another problem."

She pulled out the bagpipes from a basket under the counter. "I've been trying, but they won't make a sound."

He nodded.

"I asked Josiah to look at them last night. He doesn't know anything about musical instruments and didn't want to help me. Do you know why they would have stopped playing?"

Ewan's hands went into his pockets. "What have you done different?"

"Nothing. Watch."

She gathered the three drones, and leaned them against her left shoulder, slipping the air bag under her arm. She pointed the finger holed stick, the chanter, toward the ground, and adjusted the mouthpiece. She blew and the bag expanded but produced only an empty whoosh.

Kate moved her fingers over the holes. No sound, only air rushing between her fingers. If she pushed her elbow hard against the bag, the air came out faster, but the drones only emitted a low groan, hardly music and unaffected by her fingering.

"At least it doesn't hurt anyone's ears, now."

The way he said it, a sort of flippant remark, made Kate suspicious. She pushed out the air from the bag and stared at him. "What did you do to my bagpipes?"

"Do you have a piece of twine? Let me help you."

She set the poor bagpipes on the counter and retrieved a spool of hemp twine from the shelf. Ewan arranged the instrument like a skeleton on the counter, each part pointing in the correct direction. He tied the three drone sticks together, "so they'll stop flopping around," and then tugged apart the chanter.

Kate gasped. "Did you break it?"

He pulled a birch bark box from his pocket. "Here's your problem. You need a new reed."

She examined the roughly shaped bagpipe reed. No longer than her little finger, the reed part looked like two tiny fans glued together on the side with a narrow slit at the top. A piece of thread tied them together at the base of the fan and around an inch-long narrow tube.

Ewan plucked it from her hand and blew into it, producing an airy duck quack. "It works. I copied the old reed I found inside the chanter the other night. I could see you needed a new one."

He put the pieces back together. "Try it now."

He set the instrument into her arms. Tied together, the three drones no longer flopped out of control. Kate blew into the mouthpiece to fill the bag, and a wailing squeal sounded.

Delighted, Kate ran her fingers up and down the holes. The noise screeched like a wild cat and Ewan clapped his hands on his ears. "Enough!"

She let the mouthpiece drop from her mouth. "You don't like the sound?"

"No. Doesn't it hurt your ears?"

Her thick braids wound around her ears muffled the sound. Kate recognized it wasn't a pleasing tone, but she'd only blown the instrument a couple of times. What did Ewan expect?

"Wouldn't you rather play your flutes?"

Kate considered him. Ewan's fine ear enabled him to tune her reed flutes with tiny knife cuts. She loved the light happy sound of the small flutes, but these bagpipes gave her a feeling of power. The loud, uncontrolled noise, the heaving bellows, the floppy sticks, made for a physical experience. She loved the bagpipes, even if she couldn't play them yet.

"I adore my flutes," Kate said. "But I want to master the bagpipes. These are part of my heritage."

Ewan grimaced. "You have until Christmas, then, if you want to marry me. I can't live with a noisemaker that roars so loud and makes my ears hurt."

Kate laughed. "You must be joking."

Ewan shuddered. "I'm not sure."

Chapter 5

After he finished harvesting Reverend Cummings' fields, Ewan moved across the countryside: cutting, threshing, stacking, and stowing other farmers' crops into barns. Some days he teamed with Malcolm to tote loads to Clarkesville or Sterling for sale, other days he manned a pitchfork and spread straw. His strong arms grew more muscular and brown in the golden late summer. He slept well at night, exhausted from the labor.

Each morning he woke before the sun to read the family Bible and play hymns on his fiddle. The Word of God fired his brain; the music of God lubricated his spirit. By the time he reached the worksites, Ewan felt cheerful and strong, ready to take on the day with gusto.

Sundays were spent as a Sabbath rest, playing his fiddle in church, visiting with Kate and usually the officious Josiah, eating a hardy meal with the Mac-Dougalls. His money stash was growing, but not fast enough.

On Saturday nights, even though he hated to leave

Josiah visiting Kate, Ewan took to riding far into the county and playing at local harvest dances. He didn't get paid much, but every bit counted. Ewan even contemplated putting his savings into Josiah's bank. Compounding interest would help, too.

Most of Fairhope had finished the harvest by the end of October, and on the final Saturday night, Ewan stayed in town. He'd be fiddling for the local dance, and while he was part of the entertainment and getting paid to play, he'd still get to see Kate in her finery. Maybe he could even find an old timer to take the fiddle and he could steal a dance himself.

A big harvest moon shone down, and lanterns hung from the trees. A crackling fire sent friendly smoke into the air and provided coals to roast ears of corn. Ewan stepped up to the church porch. The dancing would take place in the open area in front of the church. He tuned his instrument and struck up the first dance, "Turkey in the Straw."

Folks had traveled from the outlying areas and brought picnic suppers. The dozen school children ran among the trees playing hide and seek, but when the music began, they circled back to watch the first reel.

Kate wore a red dress with a matching bow in her hair. Josiah Finch bowed, a stiff bend because he'd buttoned his tight vest all the way up. Ewan fingered the strings and pushed his bow fast in irritation. Finch might get every dance.

A bevy of young women he hadn't seen in months stood beside the porch, swaying with the music, tapping their toes, and laughing up at him. They smelled of sweet soap and flowers, a bouquet of happiness at his feet. Ewan smiled in return at their enthusiasm and hoped the young men lurking by the livery stable would get up the nerve to dance with them.

Malcolm stumbled up and reached for one woman's hand. She tittered and followed him into the reel. Ewan picked up the pace. For such a large man, Malcolm danced with nimble feet. Ewan laughed. He knew Malcolm would soon drop his jacket and turn as red as his hair from the exertion. Malcolm swung the petite girls so fast, their feet left the ground.

Ewan played favorite tunes from "Skip to My Lou" to "Barbary Allen." The dancers spun and sang as they moved across the grass. Children lined up, adults came and went, but always Kate danced before him. When he needed a break, he signaled to Mr. MacDougall, who called for refreshments.

Kate brought him a cup of lemonade. "That was so much fun. We haven't had a dance since you left. If you're here this winter, perhaps we can do this more often."

Perspiration beaded her brow and her auburn hair tumbled around her shoulders. She looked adorable.

"What do you mean if I'm here?"

In the lamplight, he saw Kate blush. "Of course you'll be here. When the cold weather sets in we can dance at the schoolhouse."

Ewan shook his head. "The grammar schoolhouse would be large enough if you pushed back the desks, but it's a ways out of town. Would people go so far when they can meet here at the church?"

"We'll ask Reverend Cummings if dancing is allowed. Are you tired?"

He grinned. "I'd fiddle for hours to watch you dance."

Josiah loomed up, tall and lanky with a sniff above his waxed mustache. "Aren't we paying you to play?"

Ewan nodded. "Back to work."

Kate caught his arm. "Can I join you? I've brought a flute."

He grinned. "You're on. 'Irish Washerwoman'?"

Dimples. "Fun!"

He began the complicated piece slowly, deliberately, as Kate found her key. She played a cane flute made from a thick reed cut that summer. The shrill sound always modulated under her breath, and he savored the string and reedy duet. After one round, he picked up the tempo. Kate kept pace, hitting all the notes cleanly and on time.

Faster.

The crowd stopped dancing to listen. Several clapped when they got to the end of the round and Kate kept up.

Faster. Faster. On the final round, she tossed back her head and laughed. "Ewan wins."

The crowd cheered.

They played several other duets together, his fiddle calling to her flute. It felt so right to make music with her, and Ewan knew the audience appreciated them. When the moon shone full on his face, he turned to Kate and winked. Flustered, she lost her place and put her fist on her hip in mock anger.

Laughter from their audience and then a shout: "We want to dance, Ewan. Stop teasing the girl. Play another reel."

Kate pretended to pout, but when Josiah stepped up and took her hand, she departed the steps for the dance area. She made a face at Ewan and then attended to her steps.

His heart swelled. It was enough.

⚬∾⚬

"You're making too much of the fiddler." Josiah held her too tight and too close on the promenade.

"If you were musical you'd understand."

"You should not make a spectacle of yourself. Just because everyone knows you, doesn't mean they approve of your behavior. He winked at you."

"I would have winked back if I knew how." Kate broke away.

"He flirts with all the girls. Look at him now."

Sally Martin and Priscilla Trenton hovered by the porch. Ewan leaned his fiddle at them as he played and grinned.

"He's friendly with everyone," Kate said.

Mary Standish approached with a cup. When he finished the song, Ewan drank it in one gulp. He tapped her chin and grinned. The young woman scurried away, giggling.

Kate burned. Should he welcome and tease those girls if he loved her?

Josiah drew her into the shadow of a stand of trees. "He's a country hick. All he knows how to do is fiddle. He can't support you with catgut and wood. Why don't you marry me and I'll take you on the train to Lincoln to hear real music."

"I don't want to marry you."

"Your father thinks different. You're young. You don't know your own mind yet."

"What does my father have to do with this? I do know my mind. I want," she caught back Ewan's name and modified her words, "to make music. You don't even sing."

He put his elbow on the tree trunk and leaned into her. "I sing at church, where it belongs. Music is for children. Adults don't need panpipes and fiddles to make them happy."

"You are misinformed," she said coldly. "Music draws me closer to God. It makes me happy. I sing all the time and play my flute and bagpipes daily. Maybe if you made more music, you'd be happier, too."

Josiah grabbed her wrist as she tried to spin away. "He has nothing. His dead parents were Indian lovers who lost their property. I can give you a future. He has nothing to give."

Kate twisted out of his grip. "Ewan has what I desire: music in his soul and love for God."

A shout went up, the dancing stopped and excited jabbering filled the church yard. Ewan tucked the fiddle under his arm and waited. Kate hurried to her mother. "What's happened?"

Mama's fingers went to her lips. "The schoolmarm ran off with a farmer from Dixon. She's abandoned the school."

"What will we do?"

Malcolm joined them. "Pa's talking to Reverend Cummings and Mr. Finch right now. The school board will have to find a replacement. They should hire Ewan. He could teach the little students."

"What a wonderful idea," Kate said. "Let's go tell them. You can demonstrate how much he's taught you."

"You think they'd hire Ewan because I can multiply?"

Papa thought Malcolm's improving arithmetic skills were the miracle he'd been praying for. She knew Ewan helped the little Cummings girls with their arithmetic. It couldn't hurt to ask.

She smiled at him across the church yard and tried to wink. Surely that's what being a helpmeet meant?

Chapter 6

Ewan cleared his throat. The eleven students regarded him with serious expressions. He already knew most of them, particularly the two Cummings girls who had walked him to school. Five boys and six girls ranging in ages from six to twelve were his class.

"I'm your new teacher. We're going to have fun learning to read, write, and do arithmetic."

Charity Cummings, six, raised her hand. "What do we call you?"

His lips twitched, but he swallowed the grin. "During the school day, I'm Mr. Murray."

Miss Hall had worked for three weeks and obviously planned her elopement. She'd left notes about the students and thus Ewan knew their abilities. The job paid twenty dollars a month, and with his savings, would put him within range of the seventy he needed to claim Kate for his bride.

He must not think of Kate. He had a class to teach.

Still, his thoughts drifted to the cinnamon-scented bag she'd pressed into his hands this morning. Charity and Grace, the older Cummings sister, had giggled when Kate darted out of the MacDougall house carrying the sack, her glorious hair drifting in clouds and her delicate feet bare.

Ewan cleared his throat again to discipline his mind. He led the students in prayer, played a hymn on his fiddle to get their souls stirring, and then asked Grace to read the Bible story. She stumbled on the name Zaccheus. Ewan noted she read without expression and with rigid shoulders. He'd have to help her; reading should be fluid and engaging.

"Please open your *McGuffey Reader* to your lesson and I'll take you in turn at the blackboard." Ewan beckoned to the two youngest children.

Ninety minutes into the morning, he had to clench his fists to keep from fidgeting. He gazed out the east window toward the prattling creek, remembering how school days lasted an eternity during his childhood. He'd loved the lessons but had yearned to escape to recess.

As he took the older boys through the arithmetic lesson on the dusty blackboard, he noted the same hesitancy Malcolm had shown. Tommy and Jimmy were smart boys, but Ewan wondered if they had memorized the answer, rather than understood the concept.

After three tries to solve the problem, he declared the lesson finished.

"Let's run around outside for five minutes."

Tommy's mouth flew open. "Short recess?"

"Five minutes. When I call, each of you should to go down to the creek and find ten small pebbles. Wash them and bring them back. I'll help you, Charity." He grasped her soft, tiny hand.

The settler who gave the land ten years before had ten children and lived on the eastern side of town. He'd been a cantankerous man and deliberately lived a fifteen-minute walk over a hill from MacDougall's mercantile, the first building in Fairhope. By the time townspeople built a new schoolhouse closer to town, too many students had reached the upper grades and filled the new building. The younger children's school remained out in the country.

Ewan nervously glanced to the rutted road leading past the schoolhouse into town. He knew the school board might not approve the surprise recess, but Ewan itched to get outside, and the pebbles would be part of the next lesson. Singing "Blest Be the Tie that Binds" under his breath told him when five minutes were up and he called the students down to the creek. They clomped back to the wooden building ten minutes later to find Josiah Fitch waiting for them.

"Good morning, students. My father asked me to stop by to see you on your first day with a new teacher."

"Why are you still in Fairhope?" Ewan asked.

"I'm on my way to the train. I stopped in to see how you're doing in your new job."

He gestured to the students. "We're about to work an arithmetic lesson. Gather around my desk." He directed the giggling children to set their pebbles in straight rows.

Josiah snorted.

Charity and Silas, the six year-olds, slowly counted their rows to make sure they had ten. Ewan directed them to take their pebbles and count them into two even piles. While they counted, he showed the remaining nine children how multiplication worked.

Two girls hesitated. They didn't want to get their hands dirty, but the boys seized the idea. Tommy reminded Ewan of Malcolm, grabbing pebbles and putting them into the appropriate piles. Ewan finally stood back and let Tommy show the other students how it worked.

He glanced at Josiah, who returned a sneer. "You teach school by letting the children play with rocks?"

"Only to get the concepts down."

He showed the youngest children how to add simple groups of pebbles.

When the wall clock showed noon, Ewan sent the students outside to eat dinner. He grabbed his sack and followed them with Josiah trailing behind.

Josiah clasped a hat onto his head and untied his horse. "I don't give you much hope for success. My father said if they're not ciphering by the end of the month, he'll have you fired." Josiah patted his pocket. "I've got his letter here, ready to be sent back east looking for another schoolmarm. Women do better with small children anyway."

The proverb the class had read that morning and copied onto their slates flashed through Ewan's mind: "A soft answer turneth away wrath"

He took a deep breath and quickly counted to ten. "Why don't you like me, Josiah?"

Josiah swung onto his horse and bent down to Ewan's eye level. "Because you have ideas above your station, fiddler boy." He kicked the horse onto the road to town. A cloud of dust remained behind.

Ewan shook his head and joined his students. He could hardly wait to devour Kate's treat.

⟨∞⟩

Malcolm had advanced to long division—he and Ewan

worked together two nights a week on arithmetic. Papa watched with a mixture of pride and astonishment as they scratched on slates around the kitchen table. Kate embroidered a collar for her dress and talked with Ewan in between problems.

She basked in his happiness about teaching school, delighted to be a helpmeet to a young man so enthusiastic about his job. He loved all her suggestions, particularly having the students memorize poetry. "Musical words," he called poetry, "perfect for making reading fluid."

Once Malcolm finished his problems, Kate and Ewan retrieved their instruments and played music together. The evenings always ended on a merry note, even though Ewan refused to let her play the bagpipes in his presence. It was the only discord between them.

Other than Josiah, of course.

She could never explain about Josiah to Ewan, who grew stormy-faced whenever Josiah appeared or was mentioned. Wasn't it obvious she preferred Ewan? Didn't he know she loved him alone?

Malcolm often slipped outside to give them private time, but Papa usually stormed in before they could exchange many intimacies.

"It's for your own good," Papa said one night after

Ewan left. "Until the boy shows me his hard-earned cash, you're not betrothed. I gave Josiah my word."

Kate clenched her jaw. "I told Josiah no. I'm the one getting married, and I know who I love."

"You can't live on love, girl. He needs to be able to support you."

"He works hard."

Lines crossed Papa's forehead. "I know. He's using new-fangled ways, though, to teach arithmetic and Sam Finch doesn't like it."

"If it works, why does it matter?" Kate asked.

"He's one-third of the school board. We'll have to see how much the students learn."

While chilly mornings were the norm and rain blew in frequently, surprising days of warm sunshine appeared in early November. Kate untied her apron one afternoon and excused herself from the mercantile. She and Malcolm were joining the grammar school students on an outing. Ewan needed their help.

Malcolm carried two sharp knives from the kitchen and a basket of Mama's warm biscuits. As they walked down the hard-packed road lined with fields gone to straw now the harvest was done, he muttered division problems under his breath. "Do you know how easy it is to divide by ten?"

"You take away the zero or you move the decimal point." Even as she said the words aloud, a memory tugged at her mind. Kate frowned. Had she seen a similar mistake somewhere? At the mercantile?

They heard the fiddle before they reached the school, and Malcolm chanted the times tables to the tune. They rapped on the door, and Grace Cummings let them in. Once the students and Malcolm reached "twelve times twelve is one hundred forty-four," Ewan finished the song with a nimble run up and down the fiddle strings. "Time to visit the creek."

Ewan led them around the schoolhouse and down to the water.

Tall willows sagged above the stream along with hickory, walnut, and fading wild plum trees. The hawthorn trees had lost their yellowed leaves and reached like spindles to the sky. The creek took a wide swing below the schoolhouse and reeds grew thick. Ewan directed the children to remove their shoes.

"We've come to make reed flutes," Kate explained. "My brother and I will do the cutting and whittling, and then teach you how to blow. Find a reed about this long." She held her hands eighteen inches apart.

Tommy Miler stepped into the water and pointed at a reed. With a sawing motion, Kate cut it clean.

Malcolm did the same while Ewan showed the children how to rub the ends of their reeds in the rough sand, "to smooth."

When they had their reeds, she told the children to measure two inches down from the node closing the end of the reed. "This is the mouth hole. We'll put five finger holes into your flute the width of your thumb apart."

Using the tips of their knives, the adults carved holes and rolled the flutes in the sand to smooth the cuts. They cut two pinholes in the node ending, and Kate demonstrated how to blow through them to produce a tone.

The children blew into their flutes. They positioned their fingers over the holes, and Kate helped them hear the different tones. Their eyes grew round with surprise. Several boys blew too hard, little Charity blew too softly, but after ten minutes, they all could get a clear tone.

After eating Mrs. MacDougall's biscuits, they trooped back into the schoolhouse.

Once inside, Ewan drew a picture of their reed flutes on the blackboard. "First we're going to teach you to play the multiplication song. Tomorrow we'll start on other music. It's a secret, but I'm going to teach you to play 'Joy to the World,' in time for Christmas."

Three children took to the flutes as Kate had so many years before. Others mangled the fingering like Malcolm, but their eyes sparkled. Ewan winced at some of the notes, but Kate encouraged the children to hear the changes in tone patterns. Ewan clapped, they blew, and after another half an hour, everyone needed a drink.

Ewan marked each flute and collected them into a basket. "Remember, these are a Christmas secret. Today we'll demonstrate how you can spell for Mr. and Miss MacDougall. The spelling bee commences now."

Malcolm started to protest but Kate took the proffered teacher's chair as the children lined up on either side of the room.

"Since the boys are one short, I'll join them. The MacDougalls will run the bee." Ewan took his place at the end of the line.

The girls protested, but Kate laughed. Ewan was an atrocious speller. She knew which side would win.

Unless she thought of another way to help him.

"I'll use the word in a sentence," she explained. "You'll repeat it after me then spell. Bagpipes will be the first word. 'I love the sound of bagpipes.' Mr. Murray?"

He shook his head, but spelled bagpipes successfully.

Kate laughed. "Next?"

The girls won.

Chapter 7

Ewan liked to stop at the mercantile after school to say hello to Kate. One late November day, he had a gift. Before the weather turned cold, he'd returned to the stream and fashioned three new reeds for the bagpipes.

He hoped they'd improve the sound.

Nothing could make it worse, and it was a sore spot between them. How could a girl whose flutes sang with high, silvery magic endure the raucous, out-of-control dead swan blather from the bagpipes? They'd never be a match for his fiddle's call and response.

He appreciated Mr. MacDougall's insistence she play far from civilization.

Though, of course, Ewan couldn't stay away from his pretty girl and certainly didn't want her off by herself in a field.

Ewan stuffed his ears with cotton and watched from a smug distance.

At least the bagpipes had frightened Josiah away.

The store was nearly empty on the wet day, the friendly smell of hickory wood burning in the stove making it feel cozy inside. Malcolm stacked goods on the shelves while Mr. MacDougall and Kate stared at a swirl of papers on the counter. Mr. MacDougall's lip curled up. "What made you think of this?"

"Ewan suggested if they'd made an error once, they might have done it in the past."

MacDougall scribbled down figures. He glared at Ewan. "You've seen the numbers?"

"Only those on the one bill."

The mercantile owner pushed the paper toward him. "Tote these up."

Ewan provided an answer.

"Kate says you're good at the percentage. What are they charging me per load?"

Ewan reviewed the numbers and told him.

MacDougall dropped onto the stool behind the counter and scowled at the pouring rain. "I haven't been paying close enough attention. I knew my profit was down; I didn't know why. They've been cheating me."

"For how long?" Kate asked.

"Nearly a year. Malcolm, do you want a job?"

Malcolm set the final sack of beans onto the shelf. "I'm working now."

"I need you to be my teamster. You'll drive horses to

Clarkesville next week to get our provisions. I'll let this company know their services are no longer needed." He nodded at Ewan. "Will you accompany him and figure the numbers?"

Ewan thought of his not-full-enough money pouch and sighed. He couldn't miss school to make the trip. "Malcolm can figure the bill. I'll help him unload here. I could use the work."

"Mrs. Trenton needs you to butcher her pig," Kate said. "She can't pay but she'll give you meat."

Ewan swallowed. He hated butchering animals. "Thanks. I'll talk to her."

"She wants to make sausage, so you'll need to stay into the night to tend her smokehouse. I told her you'd do it."

Ewan stared at her. "I have a job, Kate, and the school board is coming to test the students the end of next week. I need to prepare them. I may be too tired if I stay up all night tending the smokehouse."

She sniffed back tears. "But I thought you needed money. I did this for us."

"I need every cent, but I have a responsibility to the students. If they don't cipher as well as Mr. Fitch expects, I'll be out a job."

Mr. MacDougall watched him with a bland

expression. Ewan hated having this conversation in front of the school board head. "We'll need my job after Christmas to live on."

"Where do you plan to live?" MacDougall asked. "You can't expect Kate to create a home in Cummings' barn."

"Yes, where?" Kate asked eagerly. "I could be putting a home together. I could measure the windows for curtains and start sewing them now."

Ewan examined his boots.

"Are you thinking of the old soddy near the school?" MacDougall asked.

Kate's eyes widened. "Oh."

He watched Kate's enthusiasm evaporate.

Ewan put back his shoulders and faced them. "I'm fixing it up as best I can. It will be simple, but it won't be the last place we'll live. I promise."

Kate nodded, but he saw the tears building.

Ewan set the box with the reeds onto the counter. "These will help, I hope. I'll leave you to it, then."

He walked out the door into the rain and felt his spirits slip down his cheeks into a puddle of mud. He still wasn't sure where he'd earn all the money. If it meant staying up all night to earn Kate's hand, he'd do it. A squealing pig couldn't be any worse than Kate's bagpipes.

∽

"Josiah offers a warm wood house in Clarkesville. You'd have a fancy carriage, fine clothing, and a place in society."

"I don't care." Kate stamped her foot.

"We like the boy, we know he's a hard worker, but he's got nothing anchoring him. Do you really want to live in the old soddy?" Papa smacked his big hand onto the counter.

"No," Kate sobbed. "But it won't be forever. Ewan's clever and smart and I love him. It's not his fault his parents died."

"Caring for the least of them is what Bonnie did." Mama had entered the store. "We should all be ashamed. The Murrays gave their lives nursing those Indians and asked for nothing in return. We could have died of diphtheria, too. We owe the young man a little help."

Kate dabbed at her eyes. "Mama agrees. Can't we help him?"

"This is not easy for me," Papa said. "One day you'll have children of your own and you'll understand. We have to look at facts. I'd be a poor father to let you live in a dirt hut when you could have a comfortable home."

"What did you have when you came to Nebraska? You didn't always own a fine store. Guiddame told me stories about the hardships your family suffered. Why can't you give Ewan the benefit of the doubt? I'll be his helpmeet. We'll work together."

"Making music? You'd be like the grasshopper who plays away the summer to scramble in the winter and beg for help. I won't see my only daughter reduced to poverty when she has a perfectly eligible suitor asking for her hand."

"A boring, opinionated man who looks down his nose at everyone. You would shackle me with a Josiah Finch who thinks music belongs only in the occasional hymn at church? I'd rather die than marry a man like him."

Papa stood up. "You don't know what you're saying. You're being childish."

"Josiah always calls me childish. I'm not a child. I'm a woman who loves a hardworking man and I resent your attempts to marry me off to a . . ." she stuttered, "a pompous banker like Josiah Finch."

Mama put out her arms, and Kate went into her comforting embrace. "You've seen his skill with numbers, Duncan. You know how well he's done with Malcolm. Reverend Cummings cannot speak more highly of him. It will do Kate good to make a simple home at first. She needs to learn how to manage on what her husband can bring."

"In a soddy in the winter? Have you gone mad?"

"Ewan has different prospects than Josiah. He has a winning personality, excellent taste in music, and a heart for the Lord." Mama rocked her.

"That ought to count for something," Malcolm said.

"Exactly. Maybe another place will come up before Christmas, but in the meantime, he's looking ahead and preparing what he can afford. You can't fault him, even if it isn't where you would want to live. The question is, will Kate be happy there?"

Kate closed her eyes and breathed in her mother's fresh-from-the-baking yeasty scent. She tried to imagine life in a dark soddy far from town. The snug sod house wouldn't have room for anything save a stove, bed, and table. It couldn't be much larger than her bedroom.

They wouldn't have much, but every night and day Ewan would be there. He would play his fiddle and she would sing and they'd bring beauty and happiness even into the most humble home. God would be with them, and that was more important than anything. Confidence stirred in her heart.

Kate raised her head. "I can do it. I can be happy as long as Ewan is there."

Mama touched her cheek and kissed her on the forehead.

Papa scratched the top of his head and pulled his hair into tufts. He rose and paced. He smacked his right fist into his left hand and muttered.

Kate, Malcolm, and Mama looked between themselves in confusion.

"What is it, Duncan?" Mama asked.

"I cannot give my permission or blessing or help. A deal's a deal," Papa finally said. "We'll see what Ewan's made of first."

Chapter 8

The three school board members filed into the schoolhouse: Mr. MacDougall, Mr. Finch, and Reverend Cummings. Josiah Finch slunk in behind them and Ewan frowned. He'd been praying about his attitude toward Josiah when he'd realized with a sinking spirit that for Kate's sake, he needed to make peace with the man.

Ewan's money purse wasn't as fat as it needed to be for him to earn Kate's hand in twenty-two days.

He'd taken to going door to door at farmhouses outside of town looking for odd jobs after school. Reverend Cummings had paid him a small amount for whitewashing the inside of the church and for chopping firewood, but the minister didn't have much money himself.

Malcolm had volunteered to give him funds, but Ewan shook his head. A deal was a deal. He needed to earn the money.

Ewan wasn't sure what he could do. He'd have to trust God to provide for him and Kate. It felt a little too thin for comfort, however. Worry wouldn't help; he'd let the day's cares take care of themselves.

Today he needed to support his students. He nodded to the four men and introduced them to the class.

"This will be akin to a spelling bee," Sam Finch explained. "We will provide the arithmetic problems, and you will answer them. We will begin with the youngest students."

Charity and Silas stepped to the board. Mr. Finch directed Josiah to write the problems. Reverend Cummings' warm smile helped calm the children and Ewan.

The first two children worked their way through simple addition problems without any difficulty. Charity stopped and counted on her fingers twice, but the men smiled indulgently. Silas surprised them when he asked for a double digit problem, probably to show off. Josiah wrote the numbers, and before Silas could answer, Charity called it out.

The school board members chuckled. "Thank you," Mr. MacDougall said. "The next class, please."

"Why are those boys fidgeting?" Mr. Finch asked while Tommy and Jimmy worked on multiplication.

"I suspect they're singing under their breath," Reverend Cummings said.

"Singing?" Mr. Finch's voice rose.

"Speak up, boys," Mr. MacDougall said. They sang the times tables to him as they worked the problems. Their long division skills were not as strong as their multiplication, but they found the correct sums. The girls were just as good.

Two hours in, Ewan insisted on a recess. He followed the children outside into the chill air and watched them run around. He thought they'd done well, but there was no telling what the Finches would say. He muttered a quick prayer about his attitude. If he couldn't earn enough money, Kate would become Mrs. Finch. Ewan needed to be happy for her prospects.

Even if the idea broke his heart.

As he expected, when they returned to the schoolhouse, the board had made their decision. Two to two, Finches versus MacDougall and Cummings.

"Congratulations, Mr. Murray." Mr. MacDougall shook his hand. "Your students have learned a lot of ciphering. Your methods may have been unorthodox, but you have taught them well. We look forward to your return to the school after the Christmas holidays. The parents expect to hear a poetry recitation soon, I understand. You've done well."

The men put on their hats and coats and shook his hand. Reverend Cummings was the final one.

"But the vote was two to two," Ewan whispered.

"Josiah isn't on the school board," Reverend Cummings said. "You're a good teacher. Keep up the good work."

∞

In the December cold, Kate brought her bagpipes to work. As long as no one, particularly her father or Ewan, was in the mercantile, she could practice.

She'd experimented with the different reeds Ewan carved for her and found one produced a better sound than others. She'd learned how to modulate her breathing and pressure on the bag to release air into the pipes. Sometimes the clashing sounds sounded like music.

"You're getting better," Malcolm said. "I could almost hear the melody."

Malcolm still worked in the mercantile on the days he wasn't hauling goods. He'd grown a bushy beard, and the rest of his face turned red whenever Sally Martin stopped by. On slow days he pulled out a slate and worked math problems. Ewan had found a book of Euclidean geometry, which Malcolm said made better sense than long division.

As the days grew shorter, Ewan's visits became abbreviated. Kate didn't know how much money he still needed to earn and she didn't ask. When he came by, she put away the bagpipes and pulled out one of the reed flutes. The man she loved was discouraged, so she played to cheer him up.

That afternoon he shuffled in as she filled a jar with striped Christmas candy. She set it on the counter and pasted a bright smile on her face. She'd finished sewing her dress. Should she tell him?

His sad smile resembled a grimace as he tapped his long fingers on the jar. "When I was a boy, this candy meant Christmas. Ma called them Yule logs painted in Christmas colors to celebrate the holiday. I've since learned Yule logs burn in the fireplace, but seeing this candy is a happy memory."

Kate plucked a piece out of the jar and handed it to him. "Merry Christmas."

He clutched the candy and recoiled. "What's the date?"

"December 15. You have plenty of time."

Ewan opened his fist and stared at the candy, now crushed. He scooped it into his mouth, his hand shaking.

"Are you okay?" Kate reached for him.

He rubbed her hand clutching his arm. When he'd finished the candy, he cleared his throat. "'In the world ye shall have tribulation,' Jesus said, 'but be of good cheer; I have overcome the world.' I remember that verse when I'm discouraged. Ten days. God will have to do a miracle. I've been praying for Josiah."

"Why?"

Ewan lifted his head and gazed at her with those clear blue eyes. "Because I love you and I want only the best for you. If you married Josiah instead of me, you'd be safe and could have a good life. So, I've been praying he'll become the man you need him to be."

"You needn't bother. I love you, no one else. If I can't have you, I won't marry. I'll stay here and work in the mercantile. This isn't the end. If you don't have the seventy dollars by Christmas, you'll earn it next month at the school. Please don't be discouraged."

Ewan shook his head. "He said your eighteenth birthday, December 25. We gave each other our word. How could I look your father in the eye after I pledged to meet his requirement?"

"If you truly loved me, you wouldn't care. There are other ways to come up with the money. Can you sell one of your possessions? I'll buy something from you. What do you have?"

"Here. I owe you money." Malcolm rose from his chair at the back of the store. He handed Ewan two silver dollars.

"What's this for?" Ewan stared at the heavy coins.

He held up *Euclid's Geometry*. "My book. How much will you charge to curry my horses? How much do you need? I don't want Josiah Finch in my family." Malcolm walked out the door and slammed it after him.

They were alone. Kate came around the counter and took Ewan's face in her hands. "Ten more days. Mama, Malcolm, and I are rooting for you. God will provide."

"Thank you," he whispered. Ewan's arms came around her, and the kiss was worth all the anguish.

Maybe even better than making music together.

Chapter 9

Ewan tossed the last log into the schoolhouse stove. He planned to borrow Malcolm's wagon after school and haul firewood. A teacher's job involved more than classwork in Fairhope's school.

He didn't remember being so chilled while attending classes. Of course, he'd shared a desk and students huddled together when they felt cold.

"Okay, let's try it again. Top left index finger on the front hole, blow through your flutes, and let's play 'Joy to the World.'"

It was a tricky song with only five holes to play, but Kate had carved holes in the back of the flutes and shown the children how to place their thumb over half the hole, which gave them an octave-higher sound. It also turned the flute into a sharp whistle the boys enjoyed too much, but Ewan had convinced them to play softly for the Christmas carol. He knew their parents would be surprised and pleased.

The children had written poems in honor of Jesus' birth, and they had memorized the second chapter of the Gospel of Luke. Ewan planned to purchase a stick of Christmas candy for each of them with his limited resources. He was going to miss the mark to satisfy Mr. MacDougall, and eleven pennies wouldn't make much of a difference.

"In everything give thanks," he whispered. Ewan had taken to quoting scripture when he felt discouraged.

"I'm cold, Mr. Murray." Grace Cummings shook. "Can I put on my coat?"

"What happened to the window?" Tommy asked.

So caught up in the lesson, Ewan hadn't checked the window lately. Like the rest of the class he stared. It was perfectly white, as if someone had whitewashed the panes.

He peeked out the door. Whiteout conditions. He couldn't see any farther than the end of the porch. He slammed it shut. Eleven pairs of frightened eyes stared at Ewan.

You could hear rain pounding on the roof and bouncing off the stove pipe, but not snow. Snow came on quietly, tumbling from the sky in soft, fat flakes that landed as gently as a feather. They hadn't heard a sound.

Ewan's mind raced. The last wood already in the fire, the room cooling rapidly, town a ten-minute run in good weather, but not in bad. He had eleven children to care for. Would anyone come to help?

"We need to pray." He called the children together, and they knelt in a circle. "Dear God, the snow makes it hard to see. Please give us wisdom and help us make it safely back to town. Amen."

"Amen."

Surely, someone would come for them. Should they stay? But it would be dark soon. If they could find their way to the road not twenty feet away from the north end of the schoolhouse, they could follow the ruts into town.

"Put on all your warm clothing and huddle together," Ewan said. He had an axe, a coil of rope, and eleven children.

And eleven flutes.

Staying made more sense. He stuck his head out the door again. He could make out the bush beside the road. He jerked up his head. What was that sound?

Ewan grinned in relief. "Grab your flutes and get into a line. I'm going to tie you together."

He put little Charity and Silas in the front and Tommy at the end. "We're going outside, and you need to blow your flutes as loudly as you can. Turn them into whistles. We'll walk together to the road and head to town. You make as much noise as you can, then stop to listen to with me."

They stepped out slowly onto the porch, Ewan leading Charity and tugging the rest behind. He could not risk losing anyone in the swirling white. "Blow," he shouted.

They blew, high and loud.

He waited.

A honking, screaming, squabbling noise responded. Bagpipes! Ewan turned his face in the direction of the sound. "Let's go. Pipe."

They shuffled through the snow, already three inches deep, and the cold seeped into their feet. Charity clutched his hand and blew her whistle. He did the same.

Honk. Squawk.

Ewan walked in the direction of the sound. When he tripped on a furrow, he knew he'd found the road.

"Pipe!"

Eleven whistles. Ewan added a twelfth. "Silence."

The shrill trembling noise sliced through the falling snow, calling like a beacon. Ewan pulled the roped children in the sound's direction.

So they went for an endless time in freezing solid white. The snow fell upon them like shawls, blowing into their faces and clinging to their clothing. The pattern remained. Whistle, pause.

Bawl, shriek, screech.

Shuffle, shuffle, whistle.

Peep, shrill, squeak.

Tug, trudge, stumble. Whistle.

The piping slit through the snow like a knife, and the answering yammering squeal beckoned them.

By the time the first building appeared, a shroud of darkness in the impossible white, Charity and Silas were crying. Tommy and Jimmy, however, hooted when they weren't piping, and soon the answering honking oinking squeal was loud. Never had he been so happy to hear an off-key note sounding more like a bleat than music.

Malcolm reached them before they stumbled to the steps of the mercantile. He scooped up Charity and blundered into the rope, falling with a yell.

Up on the covered porch, Kate dropped her bagpipes and shouted for her father. Mr. MacDougall, Reverend Cummings, and two farmers ran out of the store. They seized the children and carried them into the warm room, where Mrs. MacDougall waited.

"God be praised," she cried.

Ewan sighed as he sank to the wet, snowy floor. "Amen."

❦

Kate shivered violently when she entered the mercantile. She felt frozen, and her lips ached. The warm air entered her sore lungs and she gasped in great gusts. The bagpipes clattered beside her into a blubbering whoosh. She felt dazed from the exertion. Where was Ewan?

"Share my cup?" Covered in snow and with blue lips, Ewan croaked his invitation. He held a tin cup to her lips filled with hot tea, but she barely registered the warmth.

"Ewan, get by the fire." Mama bustled up with another cup and a blanket. "You'll both have frostbite before this day is done."

Ewan's voice cracked. "Only if my favorite bagpipes player will join me."

Malcolm picked up Kate and carried her to a bench beside the fire where she joined the children and Ewan. They'd removed their sodden garments and huddled together, trying to get warm. The adults pressed hot tea to the children's mouths and held them close while everyone told their story.

Ewan put his arms around Kate and kissed her forehead. "How did you think to play those pipes? We wouldn't have found our way without them."

"I was practicing and noticed the snow coming down," her teeth chattered. "I didn't think much of it until Reverend Cummings came in looking for Malcolm. He wanted him to take his wagon to get the children. When we saw how fast it was coming down and how little we could see, I remembered how sound carried. I thought if I played, you might hear me."

"I wouldn't have left if I hadn't heard you squawking. You saved us. We might have frozen in the schoolhouse."

"Or you could have lost all those children on the road," Mr. MacDougall said. "You took a mighty big risk."

"I took a calculated risk," Ewan said. "The bagpipes could bring us home as long as Kate played them. You must have heard our piping?"

"Not at first. I was about to give up when I heard the whistle. I recognized it and kept playing."

"You're my heroine." Right in front of her father, Ewan kissed her.

"I'm your helpmeet." Kate laughed with relief. "After all that bagpiping, I was afraid my lips wouldn't work!"

Ewan rubbed his cheek against hers. "Your lips work just fine."

Chapter 10

The snow fell for two straight days, and the school board declared school finished until the New Year. Ewan traipsed from house to house in Fairhope looking for anyone to hire him to do anything. On December 23, he cleaned his fiddle for the last time, wrapped it in the newly washed and pressed white cloth, and closed the case.

He tucked the worn purse with $66.78 into his pocket and stepped out into the shining afternoon. Ewan had only one hope, and a faint one.

The entire MacDougall family was in the mercantile when the tiny bell rang his entrance. He nodded at Mrs. MacDougall and Malcolm, gazed a moment at Kate, and then extended his hand to Mr. MacDougall. "I've come about our deal, sir."

"Very good. Do you have the money to show me?"

"No, sir. I'm a little short, but a deal is a deal. I wonder if you would buy my fiddle for five dollars. I'd have enough then."

MacDougall crossed his arms. "I don't have any use for a fiddle."

"Papa," Kate cried. He put up his hand to silence her.

Ewan swallowed. "Malcolm, would you like to buy my horse?"

Malcolm bolted upright. "Yes! But I don't have any money, I just bought new harnesses."

"Do you have $3.22?" Ewan kept his eyes on Mr. MacDougall.

"No."

"How would you earn your keep," MacDougall asked, "if you sell the two assets you need to work?"

"Do you have any job I could do to earn $3.22 by the day after tomorrow?"

Duncan MacDougall looked him up and down. "Josiah Finch was in yesterday telling me about his house in Clarkesville and all the plans he's made to wed Kate. Do you know what I said?"

Despite his curdling stomach, Ewan answered as calmly as he could. "No, sir."

"I told him Kate had a better offer. My answer to him was no."

Kate gasped.

"Josiah Finch could give Kate a houseful of possessions, but he can't feed her soul. He can't give her the music she craves. He's a taker, not a giver."

Ewan willed himself to remain steady. "What about our deal?"

"The way I see it, there's two ways to make money. There's the money you earn and then there's the money you don't spend. Do you understand what I'm saying?"

"No."

"The Good Book says a worker is worthy of his hire. A man deserves decent pay for hard work. You saved eleven children from freezing in the schoolhouse. You led our church in worshipping God with your fiddle."

"Kate saved the schoolchildren," Ewan said. "She made their flutes and called us with her bagpipes."

MacDougall pulled a handkerchief from his pocket and wiped his face. A log shifted in the stove with a crunch, and the hot cider pot on top bubbled.

"A joint effort. You taught my son how to cipher, and by helping us find the errors with the haulers, you gave him a profession," the mercantile owner said. "But more importantly, you make my daughter happy and she loves you. I'd be a fool not to count your bill paid in full."

Ewan stood tall and smiled at Kate, who gazed back with proud adoration.

"Except," MacDougall said, "we had a deal."

Ewan's heart sank.

"Oh, Duncan," Mrs. MacDougall cried. Kate cleared a sob from her throat.

MacDougall reached under the counter. "I have an envelope for you from the school board. Sam Finch wanted you to have it after your students' impressive display last week."

Ewan slit open the heavy envelope. Five silver dollars fell out. His lips parted and he stared, first at MacDougall and then at Kate.

"After Josiah left, the school board voted again. Sam Finch, like me and Reverend Cummings, is no fool. Your new-fangled methods may not make sense to us, but those students have a stronger grasp of ciphering than they ever had before. You've earned a Christmas bonus from all of us, Ewan." MacDougall began to laugh.

Kate squealed and shuffled into a little dance.

"Your hard work earned Kate's helping hand. She's all yours, a bagpiping, helpmeet of a bride. Tell him about your dowry, Kate."

"While my dress is made in MacDougall tartan and I'm ready to wed, I've been practicing how to be a good helpmeet."

Ewan thought of the teaching job and the smokehouse meat he'd helped prepare and nodded.

"While you've worked so hard to prove yourself, I've put up food from the harvest and bought winter supplies from the mercantile. We won't starve."

"I only have $71.78 to my name," Ewan laughed. "But I have a heart full of love and music for you. Will you marry me?"

"You realize if we wed, you have to take the bagpipes, too?"

Ewan took her in his arms for a confirming kiss.

He didn't really care.

Kate was worth any sort of music: fiddling, fluting, singing, or squawking—as long as she was his.

"Is that a yes?" Kate dimpled and batted her beautiful eyes.

"I love you and your bagpipes." He laughed again and kissed his Yuletide bride. "Yes."

About the Author

Michelle Ule took her first piano lesson at the age of six and has been playing musical instruments ever since, usually woodwinds. She even marched in the UCLA Band! These days, she sings in the choir and plays her clarinet at church. Despite all her musical experience, Michelle has the worst arithmetic skills in her family—for whom she bakes a Ule log cake each Christmas in northern California. You can learn more about her at www.michelleule.com

Also from Barbour Books...

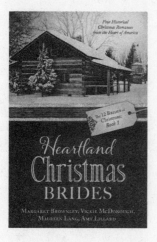

Heartland Christmas Brides

Christmas Wedding Bell Brides

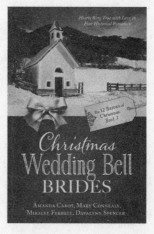